Sail Away
Home

MYSTERIES *of* MARTHA'S VINEYARD

MYSTERIES *of* MARTHA'S VINEYARD

Sail Away Home

CARA PUTMAN

Guideposts

New York

Life's roughest storms
prove the strength of our anchors.

—Unknown

CHAPTER ONE

Priscilla Grant adjusted the brim of her gardening hat to shield her eyes from the sun. The spring breeze cut right through her light jacket as it swept off the bay and over the narrow beach to Misty Harbor Lighthouse. She could taste the salt in the air. Now that the calendar had turned to May, it was finally time to plant flowers, and this year she wanted to try something new. Inspired by a gardening lecture at the Vineyard Haven Public Library, she had purchased a flat of indigenous plants in hopes of creating a more natural landscape.

The presenter had insisted that the local plants would help sustain the ecosystem of the island. While she wasn't sure about that, Priscilla loved the idea of using plants that were hardy enough for the island's swings in seasons.

The flat of plants she'd purchased at the Vineyard Gardens Nursery in West Tisbury didn't look like much now. But, in her mind's eye, she could picture the black-eyed Susans and echinacea in full bloom.

She glanced at the sketch of where she wanted to plant each one and then laid the containers out. The sun slipped behind a cloud, and she shivered as she knelt on her gardening pad. She picked up her trowel and set to work.

When she finished her planting, Priscilla stood and arched her back in an effort to ease some of the tension that had collected from bending over the bed. She kneaded her lower back and glanced at what she'd accomplished. Next, she would replant her flower boxes with rose-toned geraniums and neon pink-and-green elephant ears that would rise from the boxes while deep purple lobelia spilled down the sides. The blooms in the boxes always reminded Priscilla of her aunt Marjorie, who had left her the lighthouse at her death.

The sound of tires crunching down her driveway caught her attention, and she glanced up. Gail Smith's bright blue sedan rumbled down the gravel and pulled to a stop in front of the garage. A moment later her cousin emerged from the car, her chin-length brown hair held out of her face by a scarf she wore like a headband in a style reminiscent of Jackie O. "Priscilla, you will not believe what I just heard."

"What's that?" Priscilla asked.

Gail moved around her car and came to stand on the pavers leading to the front door. "It's so fun."

"I'm sure it is." Priscilla couldn't hold back the grin her cousin's excitement tugged from her. "Want to tell me what it is?"

Gail took a breath. "*American Antiques* is coming to the island."

The show was produced out of the Boston public television studios, but traveled around the country hosting events. Priscilla had caught a couple of episodes after Gail and Trudy talked about a discovery revealed on one. Someone had purchased a framed print for five dollars at a garage sale. When they brought it to the show, the hosts discovered a letter written from John Adams to his love, Abigail, behind the frame. That letter was worth thousands.

The cousins had buzzed about what it would be like to discover a treasure like that amid someone's junk.

"Ready to discover a letter like the one they found from Abigal Adams?"

"You know it." Gail sighed and deflated a bit. "But those kinds of things don't happen to me."

"Maybe this will be your lucky chance."

"Maybe." Gail's enthusiasm returned, and she practically bounced on her toes as she stood in front of Priscilla.

Priscilla tugged off her gardening gloves and tossed them on the ground next to her spade. "When is this auspicious event?"

"In a week. Can you believe it? They're only giving us a week to find something worth appraising."

"Should be plenty of time."

"In between my job and caring for Dad? I doubt it." Gail shifted and turned on her most imploring look. "I don't suppose you could come help me?"

"With your closets?"

"No. My friend Wanda Shire has asked me to go through her rental place to see what we find. It's the strangest thing. She got a postcard in the mail from someone who stayed in her cabin awhile back. The person said they saw something there that would be perfect for the show. But Wanda's laid up in the hospital, recovering from hip-replacement surgery. She'll be out in a day or so, but

she won't be up to digging in closets and drawers by next week."
Gail glanced from Priscilla to the gardening debris around her feet.
"I guess this isn't a good time though."

"It can be." Priscilla knelt down again. "I'm about done here. I
just need to clean up my mess." The window boxes could wait
another day to be planted, especially since Teresa Claybrook didn't
have a lighthouse tour group coming until next Tuesday.

Gail nodded. "I'll keep you company." Together, they collected
the gardening tools and empty pots and deposited it all on a shelf
in the garage before going back to the cottage.

"Give me a minute to wash up and change into something
more presentable," Priscilla said as she poured Gail a cup of coffee.
"Then we can go."

The sun had come back out when the cousins climbed into
Gail's car for the drive to the Martha's Vineyard Camp Meeting
grounds. Originally known as the Old Wesleyan Grove, the iron
tabernacle that stood at the center of the grounds had been in use
since 1879. It was surrounded by thirty-four acres that were dotted with adorable, vintage cottages. Each tiny home was covered in
weathered shingles with brightly painted porches and windows.
The site was a short walk from the Oak Bluffs Harbor area, and
Priscilla had walked it a couple of times but never ventured inside
one of the privately owned cottages. The Cottage Museum gave a
glimpse into what the cottages might look like, but it had been a
taste that only whetted her appetite to see more.

Because parking was extremely limited in the camp, Gail
parked near the dock, and then the two walked in the pleasant

sunshine onto the campground. The campground was still, nothing like how it would look and sound once the summer season started on Memorial Day weekend.

Gail led the way to a gray-shingled cottage that had yellow trim around the windows and a pitched roof, with green supports for the roof overhang. White and yellow posts supported the wraparound porch, and someone had already filled the flower boxes with plants. The sign above the front door labeled it as The Relic.

Priscilla paused across the street to take it in. "This is adorable."

"They all are." Gail dug through her purse until she pulled out a flamingo keychain. "Wanda asked me to take a look around. I suppose we could start on the porch and see what catches our eye."

"We just have to think like Tim and Cherish." The hosts of *American Antiques* made a show of finding the hidden treasure in the midst of the random collections people brought to wherever the show was filmed. "Do you think they get along in real life?"

"I guess we'll find out next Saturday." Gail stepped onto the porch and moved to one side as she scanned.

"Where are they hosting the event?"

"The historical museum, though I'm not sure that will be a big enough venue."

"Maybe we should recommend the theater." Priscilla had been amazed at how many people filled the foyer during the film festival last fall.

Gail shrugged as she worked her way back to the front door. "I suppose they know what they're doing."

"I'll check with Mildred." Mildred Pearson, who ran the museum, would have a plan in place to make the event sing. It was a great opportunity to gain exposure for the island's historic repository of artifacts.

The key was reluctant to fit in the lock, but Gail jiggled it until it slid inside. With a twist and a squeak, the door swung open, and the two cousins stepped into the shadowed interior. Gail groped along the wall until she found and flipped on a light. Honeyed wood floors filled the narrow room, and stained glass insets surrounded the square windows over the couch. Cheerful white café curtains covered part of the front porch windows. A colorful throw pillow sat on each side of the couch, and the side table held a lone box of tissues and magazines dated last summer.

"There doesn't seem to be much of worth here." Gail sounded disappointed as her gaze skimmed the room.

"If your friend rents it out, that makes sense. I wouldn't leave valuable things out for strangers to use." Priscilla turned to the staircase. "Let's see what's upstairs."

Two narrow bedrooms and a bathroom led off a small hall. The cottage felt like a life-sized dollhouse. In one bedroom, two twin mattresses rested on bed frames squeezed under the eaves. Colorful patchwork quilts covered the beds in a kaleidoscope of pastel colors against the butter-yellow walls. Only a clock and small light sat on the white table tucked beneath the window. A full bed rested beneath the sloped roof in the other room, a starburst quilt in blue tones covering its surface.

Disappointment oozed through Priscilla. "There must be some reason somebody sent Wanda that postcard."

Gail shrugged as she backed out of the room. "Maybe the quilts are valuable."

"Maybe." But Priscilla was doubtful. She glanced into the closet and spied a four-drawer dresser crammed into the space behind a narrow rod that sported half a dozen hangers. Maybe she'd find something in its drawers. She tugged the top one open and discovered nothing more than a thick layer of dust. The next one held a stack of towels and washcloths. The third was filled with sheets labeled as either full or twin. The bottom drawer stuck, and she had to crouch to tug it free. When she looked inside, she saw several wrapped items.

She eased each item from its covering and lined them up on the floor, a whole row of wooden children's toys. "Gail, come look at these."

But it was the item at the back of the drawer that really caught her attention.

Priscilla pulled it out, unwrapped it, and placed it on the floor next to the other things. Was this the treasure Wanda hoped they'd find?

CHAPTER TWO

The smaller items were hand-crafted wooden toys. The paint had flecked off a train engine, and a small airplane fared a little better. But the item that captured Priscilla's attention was the one she'd taken out last. A model ship. It was long, almost too long to fit in the drawer. It was also heavier than the toys, because it was made of some kind of metal. The ship captivated Priscilla as she set it on the floor next to the simpler wooden toys.

There were so many tiny details included on the surface of the ship that she was afraid to breathe on it for fear it would crack or something would break off. There was a tiny helm in the stern, and two lifeboats hanging above the port side. The ship had two tall masts with rigging and a shorter smokestack in between. Watchtowers, cabins with portholes, funnels, tiny pulleys, and countless other objects she couldn't name filled the deck. On the side of the ship were flecks of white paint—impossible to make out letters, if, indeed, they were letters at all.

"Gail?" Priscilla waited a moment, then raised her voice as she called for her cousin a third time. "Gail, I think you might want to see this."

A moment later Gail poked her head in the room. She glanced around, then down. "I didn't expect to find you on the floor."

"I might not get up too quickly, but what do you make of this?" Priscilla pointed at the model ship. "It must be almost a yard long."

Gail's nose crinkled as she tilted her head and considered the ship. "What is that?"

"I don't know. Maybe a toy?" Priscilla glanced at the wooden toys she'd also pulled from the drawer. "It was stashed in a drawer with these."

"I'm surprised Wanda left it in a drawer. Seems like something you would display on a mantel."

"Maybe." Priscilla wasn't sure what to make of the ship. The details on it were impeccable. "There are some marks on the side, but I can't make out what it says."

"What about on the bottom? Maybe someone inscribed something there."

Priscilla picked the ship up again, shifting it until she could see the bottom. "Nothing I can see, but the light isn't the best here."

"Well, it's the only interesting thing we've found so far. Let's take it back to your house, and I'll ask Wanda about it. Maybe she'll have some information that will help us out." Gail frowned as she looked at the model. "I'll keep looking."

Priscilla nodded. The truth was she didn't quite know what to look for, since she hadn't watched many episodes of *American Antiques*. Sure, she knew about the times someone had learned that what appeared to be junk was instead a veritable treasure hidden in plain view. Was this ship one of those items? Or was it a forgotten toy that had little value?

Guess they'd find out, either soon from Wanda, or on Saturday, at the show.

Of course, Gail might be embarrassed for her friend if they took an item with no real value. Priscilla picked up the wooden toys. Maybe she had cast them aside too quickly. It was possible some famous craftsman had made them. But while the duck, train, and simple airplane were charming, they didn't seem special. The paint flecked off the sides, and it even looked like the duck's nose had been chewed on by a teething toddler.

While it made the animal look well loved, it didn't add value to it unless she could somehow prove it was a famous baby who had chewed on it. She chuckled. She could picture herself trying to convince a lab that this duck might have Caroline Kennedy's DNA on it.

In the meantime, she knew a certain handsome Coast Guard captain who might have some knowledge about the model ship and wouldn't be averse to an evening spent enlightening Priscilla on any historical significance it might have.

A few minutes later, Gail was back in the doorway, her arms crossed over her chest. "I don't understand what Wanda wanted us to look for. I don't see anything that has value."

"Maybe we don't know what we're looking for." Priscilla slid the duck back in its towel wrapping and then into the drawer.

"Evidently, whoever wrote the postcard didn't give specifics, just that there might be something interesting here to get appraised."

"So they didn't give her any details?"

Gail harrumphed. "If they had, I wouldn't be here moping."

"What were you doing downstairs?"

"What do you mean?"

Priscilla gestured at her lanky cousin. "Just that you look like you've been crawling around in the back of closets or something."

"Or something. I've been trying to find access to the crawl-space. It was the last place I could think to look." Gail sighed. "I can't call Wanda and tell her I missed something obvious."

"Then let's trade places." Priscilla stood and then stooped to pick up the ship. "Maybe there's Depression glass or something similar in the kitchen."

Gail groaned. "I've already looked through every cupboard twice."

"I'm sure you did, but two sets of eyes are better than one. It's entirely possible there's a family heirloom up here staring at me. But if there is, I haven't found it."

"We're like the two blind mice trying to find something." Gail sighed, moved into the small bedroom, and eased onto one of the beds. "I just wanted to help Wanda. She's been a good friend to me over the years."

"Then we'll keep looking. We can take photos of the things we aren't sure about and do some research at home before deciding whether to take them to the show."

"We have to decide quickly. Wanda said a guest was moving in later this week. Once they're here, we won't have easy access to the cottage."

Priscilla reached over and patted her cousin's knee. "We'll do what we can. That's all we really can do." She smiled as she stood. "Besides, don't you want to look around your house too?"

Gail laughed, and it had the ring of irony to it. "Oh, I know we have nothing of great value." She shrugged. "We're simple island folks."

"That's true." Priscilla smiled as she shook her head. "It's a little strange to think that something we see all the time could have hidden value."

"But that's the point of the show. Alerting us to what's in front of us, but we haven't really seen."

"Well, then we need to get back to work to see what's right in front of us that we might be missing." As Priscilla carried the over-sized model downstairs, she wondered if she was looking for something that wasn't really there. The ship had a certain dated charm, but that didn't mean it had value. She needed to redouble her efforts to see what else she could find. There had to be something that would intrigue the stars of the show.

Tim and Cherish had specific taste but broad knowledge—at least from what Priscilla had viewed. How many years did it take to build the expertise to look at something and know its heritage and whether it had value? It seemed daunting to Priscilla. She set the ship on the worn couch and turned her attention to the kitchen.

She started with the cupboards. Each was crammed with dishes, but they looked like standard Corelle for the most part. A nice, simple white set that would be easy to replace if necessary.

Priscilla moved to the next cabinet, finding it stocked with various drinking glasses. Again, practical and easy to replace over something that would have enduring value.

Hands on her hips, Priscilla considered the other cabinets. No wonder Gail had become frustrated. The kitchen was equipped with enough for people staying for a few days or a week, but there didn't seem to be anything exceptional. She tugged on a drawer and found a hodge-podge of silverware. There was probably enough for twelve, but not all the same pattern.

Priscilla pushed the drawer closed with her hip and sighed. She really didn't know what she was looking for and had a feeling it wouldn't be a case of you'll-know-it-when-you-see-it.

She made quick work of the final two cabinets and then a handful of drawers. The counters were bare except for a toaster and a coffeemaker. While the stove looked like an antique, it probably wasn't worth dragging into town for appraising. She could imagine the looks on everyone's faces if she tried to haul it up the front stairs of the museum and then squeeze it through the front doors.

She wandered through the first floor, taking the wall hangings down and looking for anything squeezed between the print or photo and the backing. What were the odds she'd find something like a long-lost letter between John and Abigail Adams? Astronomical, but it was worth checking anyway.

She was in the middle of taking the backing off yet another hanging when Gail came down the stairs.

"What on earth are you doing?" Gail gave Priscilla her best you-are-so-in-trouble mom look.

"Just seeing if there's anything tucked in one of the wall hangings."

"Find anything?"

"Not yet." Priscilla eased the backing away and then checked a couple of layers of photos. Then she sighed and began to piece it back together. "There's nothing in this one either."

"It's time to admit we're not going to find anything, and I'll talk to Wanda again." Gail shoved her hands in her pockets and turned slowly. "If there's anything here, I'm missing it."

"Is she the kind of person who'd send you on a wild goose chase?"

"No. That's why I wanted to keep looking." Gail glanced at her watch. "We've been at it for over an hour. It's time to stop."

Priscilla moved into the small living room where she'd left the model ship. "Let's take a few photos of this, and you can send them to Wanda. In the meantime, I'll take it home. I'd really like to ask Gerald about it. Maybe he'll at least let us know what kind of ship it is. If no one claims it, Mildred might want it for the museum." She glanced around the space again. "I don't see anything else."

"I agree. We'll see what Wanda has to say about this boat, and ask if she can give us anything more specific that was written on that postcard." Gail pulled the key from her pocket. "Do you have time to come back with me in the next few days if I need to? I know that with Rachel's wedding, you have to be busy."

"Not yet. Rachel knows exactly what she wants and doesn't need much from me." Priscilla shrugged. "I guess it's a benefit of marrying when you're out of your twenties. She can handle most of it on her own." Priscilla would drop anything to help her daughter with her big day. Rachel had only to ask, but she kept insisting there was nothing for her mother to do.

As they drove back to the lighthouse, Priscilla kept a hand on the model ship where it sat on the back seat. She wanted to make sure it didn't get damaged during the drive. Something about the ship intrigued her.

The question was whether it was the something they were looking for.

CHAPTER THREE

Priscilla carried the ship into her living room and set it on top of the mantel above her wood-burning fireplace. The metal frame rested awkwardly in front of the lighthouse painting that filled the wall above. The ship was big enough to dominate the mantel, but its shape was unbalanced enough to make her hesitant to leave it there.

She wasn't sure of its value, and until she knew, she sure didn't want to risk the three-foot model plunging to the floor.

She eased it to the coffee table, and Jake scampered up and started sniffing it.

"Easy, boy. This isn't ours, so we have to be careful with it."

He didn't seem to hear her as he kept snuffling around it. What did he smell that was so interesting? It had been wrapped in a musty old blanket for an unknown period of time, but it was made of metal. She couldn't imagine it held any lingering scents, at least any that were interesting enough to cause Jake to focus so intently on it.

Gail walked into the living room, her phone held out. "Let me snap a few more photos. The lighting wasn't great back at the cottage. Once I have good photos to forward, I'll call Wanda and see what she can tell us about it."

"All right. I'll put together a quick lunch."

Gail was clicking away when Priscilla headed back to her kitchen. She loved the space with its old tea tins and windows that faced west, just right for watching the sun set. The appliances were relatively new, and she'd added a small breakfast table that was perfect for her when she ate alone.

Priscilla opened the fridge and pulled out a tub of her home-made ham salad. She'd made it the day before, and Gail loved it, making it the perfect lunch for them. She got out carrot and celery sticks and a homemade yogurt dip with hints of dill and onion. It was a new recipe she was trying in an attempt to make a healthy dip. After setting the table, she headed back to the living room. The soft murmur of Gail's voice stopped her.

"I'll send you the photos as soon as we get off." Gail paused, and Priscilla edged forward. Her cousin held up a finger, and Priscilla paused again. "Okay, talk to you soon." Gail ended her call and released a breath.

"Everything okay?"

"I'm not sure." Gail pinched her nose. "Wanda insists there was never a model ship at the house. She said she would remember something that large."

"It would be hard to ignore."

"I know. It doesn't make much sense to me, but she insists it's not hers." Gail started punching buttons on her phone. "These photos will jog her memory. Maybe she hasn't seen it in years and simply forgot."

"It's possible." Priscilla's gaze traveled to the ship. It seemed too large to simply ignore or forget, but it had been wrapped up and tucked away with some old toys.

Gail's phone pinged, and she slipped it in her back pocket. "All right. The photos are off. We can eat while we wait."

"I've got lunch set out."

"Is it your ham salad?"

Priscilla smiled at the enthusiasm in Gail's voice. "Made it yesterday." As they walked to the kitchen she explained about the dip. "I was watching a show on Food Network, and the host kept going on about how bad certain dressings are for us, while making a yogurt-based dip. Hopefully, it tastes as good as it's supposed to be for us."

"Doubt it. Healthy things usually aren't as fun." Gail mock-shuddered and leaned into Priscilla's shoulder. "But for you, dear cousin, I will try it."

The two chatted about things that were happening at Faith Fellowship Church, Priscilla's church home, Grace Community, Gail's church, and the local Daughters of the American Revolution chapter. "I heard at the last DAR meeting that there's some concern about who will help with the Memorial Day children's parade." Gail pushed her fork through the ham salad, then took a bite and released a contented sigh. "It's hard to imagine the island without that tradition."

"If they just need someone to help, why wouldn't it continue?"

"The teacher who's spearheaded it is expecting a baby any day now, so she's stepped aside this year. I guess she's been the heart and soul of it, and the task is bigger than anyone realized." Gail shrugged as she dipped a carrot stick in the yogurt. "No one realized how much was involved until she wasn't here to run it."

Priscilla nodded, though she didn't really know much about the parade, just that it was a long-standing tradition on the island. "I'm sure someone will step up to help."

"I thought so, too, but so far no one has." Gail bit off the yogurt-covered end of the carrot, and Priscilla leaned into the table as she waited for Gail's reaction. Her cousin would have one, since Gail liked to compare food to how things were when she worked at a restaurant as a teen. She picked up another carrot stick and ran it through the dip, then made a show of inspecting the taste and texture.

"The dill is a bit strong." She chewed again. "Ah, but the yogurt has just the right tang."

"Oh stop." Priscilla laughed as Gail picked up another carrot. "I'll take that as an endorsement."

"I might need the recipe."

"Sorry, but this is one of those times I riffed off a recipe and created my own blend." Priscilla swiped a celery stick through the dip and then savored the bite. "It is good. The flavors have blended since I whipped it together."

"Any time you want to make it, I'll be glad to help you eat it."

Priscilla laughed again. "Thanks for that. I'm glad we got to spend this time together."

"It was better than your original option."

"What?"

"Planting those annuals." Gail made a face as she placed her hand at her back. "We aren't as spry as we used to be."

"Well, I'm not on my way to the nursing home." Priscilla batted Gail's arm.

"That you know of." Gail winked and then leaned forward. "Do you have anything you want to take to the show next week?"

"*American Antiques*?" Priscilla frowned as she considered the items in her cottage and lighthouse. "I'm not sure. It's hard to think of anything I own that would interest anyone else. Most of my possessions have value to me, but it's probably more because I know the stories behind them than because of any intrinsic value. And the items in the museum are already shared with those who want to see them."

"That's what I thought as I looked around my place. Sure, we've had much of the furniture and things long enough for them to be antiques, but these are the well-used kind. Not worth much even at a rummage sale." Gail pulled her hands in front of her and tapped one hand on the table. "I guess that's why I jumped at Wanda's request. Those cottages have been owned by the same families for generations. If there's a treasure hidden on the island, it makes sense for that campground to be one place we'd find it." She glanced at her empty plate and then at her watch. "I had no idea I'd taken up so much of your day."

"I don't mind, Gail."

"I still shouldn't have. I guess you'll be glad when I'm back to work on Monday."

"I enjoy the time with you. There's still a part of me that feels like it's making up for fifty years of lost time with you and Joan and Trudy. I'm so glad we reconnected."

"All thanks to Aunt Marjorie leaving you the lighthouse."

"I'll always be grateful." Priscilla's life had taken such a turn from the Kansas farm where she'd lived with her husband, Gary. Aunt Marjorie's bequest arrived as Priscilla was trying to pick up the pieces of her life after Gary's death from cancer. While she had pleasant memories of the island as an eight-year-old, she'd never pictured uprooting to move there. How her life had changed from the moment she learned that the lighthouse was hers, and she'd decided to see what it would be like living on Martha's Vineyard.

"Rekindling friendships with you three has been an unexpected blessing."

"I love how God knew that we'd all benefit from the relationship." Gail slid her chair back and stood. "Let me help you clean up lunch, and then you can get back to your plants."

"All right." As the two worked, Priscilla asked about her Uncle Hugh. "Any word on when he and Marigold will marry?"

"Those two are the craziest. Dad was all excited to get married, and now that they're engaged, he's acting like they have all the time in the world."

"Do you think it's cold feet?"

"No. I think they don't want a fuss."

"So let's get them to the county courthouse and then have a small reception here or at the church for them."

Gail shook her head and put their dishes in the dishwasher. "You'd think something simple like that would work, but I can't figure out what Dad really wants, let alone Marigold. Maybe they just wanted to know that they were committed to each other."

Priscilla didn't think that was it. Then a thought struck her. "Do you think they're concerned about church?"

Gail looked at her, brows crinkled and head cocked to the side. "What do you mean?"

"Well, you and your dad go to Grace, and Tommy and Marigold go to Wesley Chapel. If they want to get married in a church, the location could be an issue."

"I suppose." Gail sighed. "I'm just so used to waving over the fence at them every Sunday morning, that I hadn't considered how that could be a problem for a wedding. Seems silly, but you might be right."

"Faith isn't silly, Gail."

"I know, but it is when you're my dad's age and letting that keep you from taking the next step in life."

"There has to be a way to help them. Maybe they could have a small ceremony and reception here." Priscilla had let people use the lighthouse grounds a few times for events. One time she'd even rented her yard and lighthouse to a movie production company. While she wouldn't necessarily want to be in charge of an event that large again, a small event for her uncle and his intended would be a pleasure. A small way to love the family that had welcomed her back to the island so thoroughly.

And as she looked at her cousin, she couldn't help wondering if helping Uncle Hugh into the next stage of his life would also help Gail decide whether she wanted to make her relationship with Tommy Townsend permanent as well.

CHAPTER FOUR

The sun was beginning to slide down the horizon when Priscilla looked up from where she was working in the backyard and saw a man walking down the beach toward her. She would know that steady gait and solid build anywhere. Gerald O'Bannon. The man she'd never expected to find when she came to the island.

Back then she'd imagined she'd be a widow for the rest of her life.

Now, as she watched him stride purposefully across the sand toward her, it was hard to believe how much she had come to rely on this man.

He was as steadfast as the sea was dynamic. He could stand like an anchor through the storms of life, and he lent her his steadiness freely. She smiled as he walked up the stairs from the beach toward her.

"Where's your boat?" The wind tried to toss her question back at her, but she knew he'd heard her by the light smile that answered hers.

"Back thataway." He came to a stop at the top of the stairs, barely breathing hard. His decades in the Coast Guard had kept him physically fit, and she knew he was the kind of man to stay active in his retirement, which was coming up in a matter of days.

She knew Gerald would continue his service to the community. The Martha's Vineyard Youth Council had approached him about mentoring at-risk and low-income youth in a program of water sports and safety classes. He was excited about this new direction in his life, just as she had been when her move to Martha's Vineyard opened up a new world for her. Life was filled with pivot points. It was all about how you chose to move through the dance. Was it a slow waltz or a fast-paced cha-cha-cha? She grinned at him.

He cocked his head to the side and smirked. "What?"

"I'm excited for you and all that will happen as you retire."

"It's like having a brand-new ship that's never sailed. I'll be taking her on the maiden voyage without a map."

"Exciting?"

"Exhilarating." He bounced on the balls of his feet. "I've known where I was going and what I was doing for most of my life. To have the opportunity to redirect as I choose is a task I'm praying over a lot right now."

"Then you'll be well prepared when the new chapter starts."

"New voyage." He winked at her, and her breath caught in her chest.

A new voyage, indeed.

He wrapped her in his arms and gave her a kiss. "Would you like to walk the beach?"

"Let me get Jake." Her dog loved long walks on the beach, but she'd had to put him inside since he'd been more interested in digging up the flowers she'd just planted. "It'll just take a minute. Would you like something to drink first?"

"That'd be nice."

They walked to her cottage, and their shoulders brushed. She liked having him near and being able to talk about their days. It didn't happen every night, but when it did, she felt more settled as she prepared for bed. There was something securing about being known by someone who wanted to see into your heart and thoughts.

Gerald followed her to the kitchen. "I'm going to have some of your wonderful iced tea. Do you want a glass?"

Priscilla got Jake's leash from its hook. "Yes, please."

Jake came bounding into the kitchen then, skidding across the floor as if to make up for lost time.

"Did we catch you napping, boy?" Priscilla reached down to scratch behind Jake's ears, and he leaned into her leg as if to say *more please.*

"Do you ever think about getting another dog?" Gerald opened a cabinet door and pulled down two glasses.

"In this space?" Priscilla gestured at the small kitchen. "It's fine for one dog and me, but I'm afraid another one would get underfoot. Look at Jake. He already likes to plant himself right where we are."

Jake moved over and stood between Gerald's spread feet as Gerald took the tea from the fridge. He filled the glasses and handed one to Priscilla.

Gerald tried to step around Jake, but the red and white dog simply moved to stay in the same basic position. Gerald shook his head with a laugh. "I see what you mean. He'll calm down eventually."

"Maybe, but I've had friends whose eleven-year-old dogs still act like puppies." She eyed her dog as she drank her tea. "I can imagine Jake falling in the eternally frisky puppy category rather than sedate middle-aged."

Jake danced to her side and then sat and cocked his head. His intelligent eyes seemed to ask, *So are we going yet?*

She laughed and hooked the leash to his collar while Gerald took a long swig of his tea, then adjusted his Coast Guard baseball hat. "Let's get him outside and stretch his legs."

They walked outside, where the evening felt peaceful, and the sun was painting the sky in soft pastels as it began its descent. The gentle breeze teased Priscilla's hair, and she inhaled the scent of the ocean. Jake tried to tug her in various directions, sniffing and snuffling his way through the sand. It was like he was on a mission to find every tiny crab buried in the sand. One of these days she expected one to clamp onto his nose, though she wasn't sure it would actually detour him from continuing his frantic search.

Gerald reached for her free hand, and she felt the warmth of the instant connection. "So how was your day?"

She filled him in on Gail's request. "We're waiting to hear back from Wanda, but the ship has me curious."

"Why's that?"

"Because it's so unique." Priscilla briefly described its size and color. "I'll show it to you. You would have a better understanding of what kind of ship it is."

"I'd be happy to look at it when we get back to your place."

"That would be great." Priscilla sighed, and he tightened his grip on her hand. "When Gail asked me for help, I thought it would be a simple treasure hunt. It didn't take long to realize that it would be more complicated than that. It wasn't like there was an item standing on the entry table screaming at us to pick it up."

"I bet not."

"Silly, huh?" Priscilla glanced at him to read his expression.

"Well, it would be nice if something like that happened."

"Have you watched many episodes of the show?"

"A few." Gerald turned toward her. "Maybe we should stream a couple of the old episodes. I've seen them on the network's website. That would give you a better idea of the hidden treasures that exist. I've got time to watch one tonight if you'd like."

"Okay." It would be interesting to watch an episode with Gerald, since enthusiasm piped into his voice as he talked about the show. "Do you have a favorite episode?"

"Well, there's one about this really unique room fan. It was powered by kerosene or propane. The fuel was in a canister at the bottom that blew the hot air up toward the fan blade to spin it. Kind of an interesting idea, but not effective since it was released around 1920, about the same time electricity was taking off." Gerald resumed walking, and Jake lurched ahead again. "But because there are so few, that odd fan was worth something like two thousand dollars."

"That's fascinating."

"There was another episode that dealt with a statue of an Egyptian god from around 400 BC. Because it was broken in half, it wasn't worth as much as it could have been." Gerald released her hand as he described the size and shape. "The owner was told to get it cleaned, and when she did it ended up selling for around $95,000."

"Wow. I can't imagine having something that old and valuable hanging around my house." She let Jake begin to tug her back to the house. "How did she come to have it?"

"If I remember correctly a relative had bought it in England in the 1910s. But I'm not certain." He shrugged and grinned sheepishly. "I guess I enjoy the stories."

"I can see why." Priscilla squeezed his hand. "It sounds fun. I can make popcorn if you can pull up an episode."

"Cut up some apples?"

"Sure. Some cheese too."

"I've always thought that was the perfect light supper." He picked up his pace, and Priscilla felt pulled by both man and dog, both eager to get back to the house.

"I won't be able to dash up the stairs, you know."

"That's all right, isn't it, Jake?" Gerald's steps slowed as they neared the stairs. "Jake and I will walk with you. It'll be fine." Something feisty had gotten into Gerald, and she liked it. In some ways he seemed more relaxed, as if making the decision to retire had freed him to enjoy life in a way that he couldn't while wrestling with the decision.

Once they climbed the stairs that connected the narrow beach to her yard, they sedately crossed the lawn. In no time, they were back inside Priscilla's cottage, and Gerald was working on connecting her TV to the show's website, while she popped microwave popcorn and sliced the requested apples and cheese. If she closed her eyes, it almost felt like similar nights back on the farm in Kansas with Gary and Rachel, but Gerald was his own person, and Martha's Vineyard was very different from the flat farmlands. She prepared a tray with their simple meal and went into the living room. She placed the tray on the coffee table and sank onto the couch as Gerald punched a few more buttons on the television remote.

"Here it is. This is an episode from the Philadelphia area." He settled back next to her. "I've seen this one, and I think you'll really like some of the historical finds. It's fascinating to watch the appraisers at work."

"Tim and Cherish?"

"Sometimes they appraise too, but they always serve as hosts. They're the consistent face of the show. Depending on where an episode is taped, the show brings in additional auctioneers and the like. Say they're in Denver, they might bring in someone who's proficient with cowboy art."

"Cowboy art? There's such a thing?"

"Of course. Remington sculptures, C. M. Russell paintings, and things like that."

"I'm kidding!" She tapped his arm. "Remember, I'm from Kansas."

Gerald leaned forward and filled a bowl with popcorn, then added more salt. He munched on a handful as the show began. Priscilla watched the episode with interest, trying to note what people had brought and what the appraisers liked. It was quite the mix of items. There were dishes, some Depression glass, and some traditional china. There was an assortment of photos and documents, and Cherish got excited when a letter that looked to be an authentic Benjamin Franklin was revealed. Her blonde bob bounced around her shoulders as she examined the letter over the shoulder of the professional. Her smile was perky and her eyes bright as she asked a couple of questions about how the appraiser determined provenance.

Then the episode ended after two paintings and a book were examined.

"Can I see the ship now?" Gerald's words caught Priscilla off guard.

"I should have thought to do that right away. I'll go get it."

She went into her bedroom where she'd put the ship on her bed, and brought it back to the living room. Gerald moved the tray, and she placed the ship on the coffee table.

He crossed his arms and leaned in to examine it. "You said this was a toy?"

"I'm really not sure." She described the dresser they'd found it in and the toys that had been with it. "What do you make of it?"

He frowned and shifted to look at it from one side and then the other. And then, to Priscilla's utter surprise, a look of delight crossed his face.

CHAPTER FIVE

G erald? What is it?"

"Well, I can't be certain, not yet. I'd have to do some research."

"Certain of what? What are you talking about?"

"I'd like to do a bit of research before I commit."

Priscilla groaned. "Really? Seriously? You're not going to tell me."

Gerald grinned at her. "Believe me, if it's what I think it is, what I'm almost certain it is, you're going to be thrilled. Let me get a few photos of it."

Gerald's phone vibrated as he pulled it from his pocket. He read the text and then opened the camera. "I'll try to do some checking tomorrow or the day after and get back with you ASAP."

"I'm going to try to wait that long, but you know I'm not the most patient person in the world."

Gerald laughed. He pulled her into a hug and kissed her. "I don't want you to be disappointed if I'm wrong. I'll let you know as soon as I'm sure. I promise."

He finished with the photos, and then walked back to the couch and began collecting the bowls and putting them on the tray.

"You don't need to help clean up."

"Sure I do. I can't have you taking care of my messes." He picked up the tray and walked back to the kitchen. "Do you have anything you want to take to the show for yourself? Did you get any inspiration from that episode?"

"I don't think so. There might be something in the lighthouse, but I'm not going to sell anything. At most it would make me nervous about whether I have sufficient insurance." She swallowed at the thought. "I'm not sure I can afford much more than I already carry. The reality is, if anything happened to the lighthouse, there's probably no way I could afford to replace some of those items, even if I could find replacements."

"It could still be interesting to hear what the appraisers think."

He sounded like he'd thought about it, and she had to know. "Do you have an item in mind?"

He leaned against the counter and shrugged as he watched her start water in the sink. "Not really. I can look through your collection if you'd like."

"Oh, Gerald, would you? That would be really helpful. Gail is going to look at her house too, but she doesn't think she'll find anything." She put the dishes in the soapy water. "I'm pretty sure I don't have much of value here in the house—unless there's another Revolutionary gold coin buried somewhere in a trunk or a famous painting hidden behind a canvas. Otherwise, pretty much the only real worth my things have is personal."

Gerald grinned. "Those were pretty stellar finds. But I understand what you mean. The Coast Guard has moved me enough that I've neither had the opportunity, nor the desire, to put much stock in things." He pushed away from the counter. "I'd better head home. There's a surprise inspection in the morning, which means I'll have to be at the station bright and early."

"That doesn't sound like much of a surprise."

"It can't be for me since it was my idea." She laughed, and he moved closer to her, within a hairbreadth. He cupped her face with his palms and kissed her. "Thanks for the walk and company tonight," he whispered. "I love you."

Priscilla felt the tingle all the way to her toes. She wound her arms around his neck and kissed him back. "I love you too. Call me when you get home?"

His grin was jaunty as he pulled his baseball cap on. "Count on it."

After he left, the kitchen felt empty. It wasn't a large room, but without Gerald and his personality, it felt spacious.

She much preferred Gerald's presence in it.

In a few minutes she had the kitchen back in order and was headed to the living room. Jake was sniffing the ship again. "Leave it alone, boy."

The dog didn't even turn to look at her, but kept on sniffing.

"I wish you could tell me what you smell. Maybe there's a clue in it." She laughed at the fanciful notion. The ship had been wrapped in an old blanket in a largely unused dresser. If Wanda didn't put it there, who did? And what kind of ship was it? She knew how busy Gerald was lately. It wouldn't hurt to do a little researching on her own, would it?

She collected her laptop from her room and curled up on the couch. As she stared at the search engine box, she wasn't sure exactly what search terms to enter first. *Three-foot ship* didn't produce anything useful, so she'd have to get more specific. As she eyed the ship on its perch, she wasn't sure how.

Then she remembered the magnifying glass that she had in her junk drawer. She set the computer aside and got up to retrieve it. A minute later she was hunched over the ship, examining it inch by inch. The problem was she didn't really know what she was looking for. There weren't any dents or blemishes, and overall it was in good condition. As she shifted it, she rapped the side of it, and there was a slightly hollow, metallic ring.

She wasn't sure what to do with that detail other than note that it wasn't wood like the toys stored with it. There was no way she could chemically test the metal. She laughed at the thought. Clearly she'd seen a few too many crime procedural shows. Those kinds of tools weren't available to someone like her, and it was overkill anyway. No matter how she scrutinized the ship, she couldn't find a name or anything that resembled a name on it.

Jake whined, and she rocked back on her heels as she rubbed his head. "I'd love to know what kind of ship this is, especially since Gerald was so excited, but I guess I'll have to wait for him to tell me."

Priscilla started scratching Jake's back, and he leaned closer into her side and sighed.

"I'm not sure I'm going to learn anything more from the ship tonight." She cocked her head and looked at it. Nothing of significance came to her. It didn't matter which way she considered the ship, it wasn't releasing its secrets.

Her phone rang, and she spent a happy thirty minutes talking to Gerald about everything and nothing. She tried to tease him into giving her more information about the ship, but he just laughed at her and told her she'd have to wait.

After hanging up she pushed to her feet, and Jake followed her the few feet down the short hallway to her bedroom. Her four-poster bed welcomed her as she walked across the bright-toned rag rug past the tallboy dresser to the small closet. She changed and walked to the bathroom to finish getting ready for bed. Then she crawled between the covers and read until her eyes grew heavy.

The next thing she knew, the shriek of her phone woke her.

She groaned and rolled toward her bedside table where she groped along it until she found her phone. She blinked, tapped the screen, and put it to her ear. "Gail?"

"Did I wake you?" Her cousin's voice was way too chipper.

"You could say that."

"Sorry, but I heard from Wanda."

"It must have been good news." Priscilla pushed to a sitting position and tried to get her brain to realize she was awake.

"Not really."

"What?"

"Wanda's never seen the ship before."

"You mean she forgot that there's a three-foot metal ship at her cottage."

Gail was silent a moment, and then Priscilla heard her concern. "No, she insists it's not hers."

Priscilla pulled her knees up and leaned forward over them. "That doesn't make sense."

"I know."

"What does she want us to do?" If it wasn't hers, how had it gotten there? "Surely, she forgot about it. We could take it to her today, so she could see it in person. It's Saturday, and I don't have much going on." In fact, she didn't have anything pressing, just more yard work.

"Maybe that's what we should do. I'm mystified."

Priscilla glanced at her clock and saw it was a bit after seven. "Pick me up at eight?"

"Okay. I'll bring coffee."

Priscilla laughed. "That would be good. See you in an hour." After she hung up, she climbed from the bed and grabbed her robe. Then she corralled Jake and led him outside, where he wandered around the edge of the invisible fence as if checking for any changes overnight before he settled down and took care of business.

She ate a quick bowl of granola and read her devotions before she got ready for the day. By the time Gail pulled into her driveway, she was waiting on the front step, enjoying the way her flowerbeds were shaping up. With a little water and some sunshine, the beds would fill with color.

After Priscilla deposited the ship in the back and nestled into the passenger seat, Gail handed her a travel mug full of coffee. "It'll take about thirty minutes to get to Wanda's house."

"Not a problem. My day is clear, so drive away, cousin."

Gail turned around and headed out on the highway. "I talked to Dad last night."

"You did?" There didn't seem to be anything unusual about that, since Gail lived with her dad.

"You got me thinking. Dad loves Marigold, and I know she loves him. He said last night they'd get married tomorrow if we could get the license and their friends together."

"That's great!"

"Except it still doesn't solve the place problem. Those two will have to sort out their congregational differences once they're married. Who knows? Maybe they'll end up at your church." Gail's nose wrinkled as she said it, but Priscilla didn't take offense.

"It's a good, solid choice, Gail."

"I know, but Dad's gone to church at the same place as long as I can remember."

"Marriage requires many compromises. They'll be fine." Priscilla took a sip of coffee. "Yum, hazelnut. So where do they want to get married?"

"The lighthouse." Gail glanced at her long enough for Priscilla to catch her tension.

She tugged her phone from her purse and then pulled up her calendar. "When do they want to do this?"

"I guess as soon as you're free, if you're sure."

"Of course Uncle Hugh can use my grounds. I'll even have the rest of my spring flowers planted in the next few days." Sooner if she didn't keep taking off with her cousin.

"It doesn't sound like they want to invite many people."

"Even if they did, we could make it work. I had two hundred for that Hollywood event. And now I know which vendors to use for chairs, tents, tables, etc." Priscilla knew this small event couldn't be as complex as that afternoon turned out to be.

"That's good." Gail said.

Priscilla couldn't help but wonder what it would mean for her friend to no longer provide care for her dad on a daily basis. "Are you ready for the freedom?"

Gail stopped at a stop sign before she turned to Priscilla. "What do you mean?"

"You won't have to take care of your dad and provide meals and things for him."

"It doesn't mean I won't check in on him." Gail smiled softly, then turned her attention back to the road and pulled across the intersection. "I'll never forget how Dad was there for me when Brett took off. I couldn't have made it through those early days without Dad's steadfast help."

"He's a keeper."

"He is, and I'll do whatever he needs. It's the least I can do after all he did for me. That's what family is for."

Priscilla nodded, understanding what Gail couldn't say. There were times in life when you needed someone to not just come alongside you, but to carry you. She herself had needed that when Gary died, just as Gail had needed it when Brett abandoned her. When family filled that role, it was a debt you would gladly pay again and again.

"Check with your dad and Marigold. When they have a date, let me know." She scrolled through her calendar for the rest of May. "Looks like I could host their event just about any day but the day of the show."

Gail pulled onto a gravel drive and bounced down it. "Wanda's house is the small one up there on the right. She said she was released from the hospital last night, so I think she'll be tired. We'll have to be sensitive to what she can handle. She's the kind of person who loves company, so she won't tell us when she's tired."

"Then we'll be easy on the interrogation."

Gail laughed as they pulled to a stop in front of a well-maintained wood-shingled home. The shingles had the weather-beaten look of those long exposed to sea salt. As they stepped from Gail's sedan, Priscilla pictured an old woman who was as weather-beaten as her house and was losing touch with her memories. How much enlightenment could a confused old lady give them?

CHAPTER SIX

A cheerful voice reached them through the storm door. "Come in."

"Were you waiting for us, Wanda?"

"I have to do something before I go crazy here." The voice gained strength. "Come on in now."

Gail opened the door. "Wanda, it's Gail, and I've got my cousin Priscilla with me. Remember, I told you about her on the phone?"

"Yes, yes. I'm in the sitting room."

Gail led the way to a room on the left. A small woman with silver hair sat inside, one leg encased in a brace, her wheelchair positioned so she could look out the window. Her face was drawn, but based on the way her blue eyes sparkled, Priscilla had to change her preconceptions. Wanda Shire was anything but confused. She reached out her hand to them. "Thank you for coming, girls."

Priscilla grinned at being called a girl as she stepped forward to shake hands with Wanda. "I like you already."

"Oh?" Wanda raised an eyebrow.

"Anyone who calls me a girl is bound to be a good friend."

Wanda smiled, and the lines around her eyes and mouth eased. "Please have a seat." As the cousins complied, she continued. "I have to say I'm very curious about your call and your photos, Gail."

"You have us curious too." Gail glanced at Priscilla, then perched on the edge of a 1960s-vintage couch with its gold and brown flowers. "We went to your cabin yesterday like you asked, but didn't find much."

"Just the model ship." Priscilla sat next to Gail and leaned forward. "I left it in the car, but it's roughly this big." Priscilla held her hands about three feet apart. "It's made of some kind of metal and has a fairly elaborate deck."

Wanda looked at her with a blank expression. "I have no idea what you're talking about."

Priscilla looked at Gail. "I'll go get it."

Gail was asking Wanda about what other treasures might be in the cottage when Priscilla returned a few minutes later. She carried the ship into the sitting room, and Wanda's eyes widened when she saw it.

Priscilla set it on the small coffee table and looked at Gail. "Like we said, we found it in the bottom drawer of the dresser in the twin bedroom."

Wanda's brows wrinkled, and she looked from Priscilla to the ship and back again. "I've never seen it," she repeated.

"It was with three wooden toys. Each was wrapped individually."

"Wooden toys? We haven't had toys in that cottage since my grandchildren outgrew them ten years ago."

"Then how did it get there? It's too big to be forgotten." Rachel had been known to forget a Strawberry Shortcake doll or Polly

Pocket in hotels when they vacationed, but the ship was too large to accidentally leave.

"Or ignored by a cleaning service worth its salt." Wanda shook her head. "I'm truly mystified. Can I hold it for a moment?" Priscilla picked it up and eased it onto Wanda's lap. The older woman considered it, but didn't try to lift it or turn it around. "You have presented me with quite a mystery. I don't know where this came from or who owned it, but I can see why you'd be intrigued by it. It looks like quite the collector's piece. The question is, who was the collector?"

Priscilla took the ship from her and placed it back on the coffee table. "Could it be someone who stayed in the cottage? Maybe they left it by mistake?"

Wanda's raised eyebrows communicated that her thoughts mirrored Priscilla's on the likelihood of that happening. "I had someone who stayed into November, but it's been empty since then."

Priscilla rubbed the back of her neck. "Wanda, do you still have the postcard you received telling you about something valuable being in the cabin?"

"Of course I do." Wanda wheeled to the desk in the corner of the living room and took a card from the middle drawer. She handed it to Priscilla.

Priscilla studied both sides. "Nothing to tell you where it came from, other than a Boston postmark. And it just says they think there's something antique of value in the cabin."

"I couldn't see anything either," said Wanda.

Gail snapped her fingers. "I remember what I wanted to ask you. What about your refrigerator? It's working, and it could be antique. It's one of those 1960s GE numbers."

Wanda laughed, and it was a delightful sound. "No. That stays in the cottage, though I like your creativity. I assume you checked the wall hangings."

"Yes. Checked between pictures and their frames too," Priscilla assured her. "Some of them had multiple photos stacked in the frames."

"That's what happens when you decorate by layering." Wanda lifted her chin. "That cottage has been in my family for four generations. Each has added to what the others left behind, but not removed much. You should have heard the squabbling when electricity was added and then the kitchen rearranged to make room for a refrigerator. My dad insisted an ice box was all that was needed for the limited time it was used."

"What changed his mind?" Gail leaned forward in a mirror of Wanda's body language.

"My mother. She insisted she wouldn't go back without a few modern conveniences. That argument had worked for one of her friends, and somehow she got my father to believe she meant every word, even though he knew she adored her weeks in that cottage. She called it pretend housekeeping." Wanda smiled, and her eyes took on a distant view. "We would spend several weeks a summer there, taking part in the tabernacle services and other social events. The kids would play on the beach and the adults would chat, read, or play horseshoes."

"It sounds idyllic." There hadn't been anything like that around the Kansas farm when Priscilla was a kid.

"Then it was my siblings and me sharing it with a few cousins. We got it a couple weeks a year, but over time, as people moved or lost interest, I became the caretaker."

Gail leaned forward and took her hand. "You've done a good job with it."

"I've let the management company do the work. I just reserve a week or two during the season to enjoy it when my kids and their families come home to the island." She shifted against the back of the wheelchair.

Priscilla glanced around. "Do you need a cushion or pillow?"

"No, I'm just tired of sitting in this thing, but it's the main way I'll get around, at least for a while."

"How long will you be in that brace?" Gail had spent one summer in a cast as a child and still talked about how much she had hated it.

"The doctor said it all depends on how fast my body wants to heal." Wanda tapped the brace. "I didn't realize that stepping off the curb wrong could do so much damage. If I was thirty years younger, he said I'd just be on a knee scooter. But thanks to my achy hip, this is what I get."

"Is there anything you need?" Priscilla had just met Wanda, but she knew what it was like to be dependent on others. "Groceries or anything like that?"

"My kids arranged for someone to come in a couple times a day to make sure I'm eating and have what I need."

"Then we'll work on this ship." Gail glanced at Priscilla. "Where do you think we should start?"

"Back at the cottage, if it's okay with you, Wanda."

Wanda waved her hands. "Sure. I'm not using it, and the management company told me it's empty until Friday. You've got a week, but you have to know what's going on by then anyway, thanks to the show. I have to know if this is the item I should show or not."

Priscilla frowned. "What do you mean? Can't you show more than one item?"

Gail shook her head. "No. The rules of the show are clear. A person can only show one item. Not only that, you have to sign a paper saying you're the owner of the item before you're permitted to show it."

Wanda nodded. "That's why we need to find out if this is something I should show, or even if I should, if I can. Or is there something else that would be better?"

"Well, then we better get crackin'," said Priscilla. "When was the last time you stayed at the cottage?"

Wanda's shoulders lifted and dropped as she pushed out a breath. "We stayed there a week in June. After that it was a day here or there when the cottage was available, but not for any length of time. The company kept it hopping."

"And you didn't notice the ship?"

"No, but I don't use that room. That's for the grandkids. Often I'll drive back and forth. There's something about being in my own bed."

"No place like home." Priscilla stood. "Thank you for your time." She turned to leave, then paused. "Do you know if the management company would let us know who's rented the cottage in the last year or so?"

"They should, but if not, have Renee call me. I'll tell her to give you whatever you need."

"Thanks."

Wanda made a move to stand, then sank back against the wheelchair. "I'm still not used to this thing." She sighed. "Thank you for helping with this. I'm certain I'd remember a ship that large. Like you said, it's too big to forget."

Gail said her goodbyes with a promise to check back in the next day or two, and then the cousins headed to the car. As Gail drove to Vineyard Haven, Priscilla glanced in the back seat at the ship.

"You know, I can't get around the fact that it's too big to leave. But it doesn't seem like something someone would hide."

Gail kept her eyes on the road as she answered. "I'm glad you're the one who likes to solve puzzles, because this is a humdinger."

Priscilla burst out laughing. "A humdinger? Were you watching old movies with your dad last night?"

"Maybe." Gail grimaced as she slowed down for a couple of bicyclists who were struggling against the wind coming off the Bay. "He's been on a *Thin Man* spree this week. Don't get me wrong. Those are some of my favorites, but I'm ready to jump back to the twenty-first century."

When she pulled into Priscilla's driveway, it was still late morning. Gail parked her car and turned to Priscilla. "What will you do next?"

"I think we should return to the campground and see what the management staff can tell us. I showed the ship to Gerald last night, and he has an idea about it, but he wants to check it out before he tells me what it is. So I think we should concentrate on where the ship came from and let him handle whether it's valuable or not." She looked at Gail. "I'd like you to come with me to talk to the management if you can, because the staff is more likely to know you."

"I need to get back to Dad."

"He's alone while you're at work all day. Isn't he used to it?"

Gail nodded. "I know you're right, but today he made me promise we'd go get his favorite lunch. Says it's past time to get him some hummingbird cake."

"Uncle Hugh has a soft spot for that." Always had. It was amazing his girth didn't reflect his love of the sweet dessert.

"He does."

"Will you call ahead for me?"

"Sure. It's probably a good idea to do that anyway. I'm not sure what the office hours are on a Saturday, if they have them. Let me get home, and then I'll look up the number. I'll let you know when I've talked to her."

"Sounds good. And don't forget to give me a date for your dad and Marigold."

Gail rolled her eyes, then grinned. "Right away, Mother."

Priscilla laughed. She climbed from the front seat before pulling the ship from the back. "I'll wait for your call."

Jake was ready for a walk when she got inside and deposited the ship. He danced around her feet as if it had been weeks since she'd taken him outside instead of earlier that morning. He went to the hook where his leash hung and whined before nosing it.

"All right, boy. We'll go out." As they walked the beach, Priscilla barely noticed that he was tugging her all over the sand as he sniffed and dug. Instead her attention was tuned to the phone in her pocket. Once she got the call from Gail she could take the next step.

She was stymied about the owner of the ship until she got permission to talk to someone in the management company. Since the ship wasn't willingly giving up clues to its identity, she'd turn to tracking down who had left it.

It was a long shot, because there was no way to know when the ship was left. It wasn't hidden, at least not very well, because anyone who rented the cottage could and most likely would use the dresser in the bedroom. So without a clear timeline, she would start with last year and work her way backward until someone remembered it. If she dug deep enough, she'd eventually find something. That was how these things worked, right?

CHAPTER SEVEN

It was shortly after one when Gail called. "Sorry about the delay getting back to you, but Dad insisted he needed lunch immediately." Gail sounded exasperated, but Priscilla could hear Gail's love for her dad.

"Was anyone at the management office?"

"Yes. The woman in the office today is Renee Overman. She planned to call Wanda to confirm she could release information to you, but seemed willing to talk to you as long as you arrive before three. She said that's when check-ins start, and it gets a little crazy." Gail rattled off the association address.

"Great." Priscilla glanced at the clock on the kitchen wall. "If I leave soon, I'll be there in plenty of time."

"Let me know what you learn."

"Of course. Talk to you soon." Priscilla clicked off the call and looked at Jake, who had plopped next to her and tilted his head as if he were following her conversation with Gail. "I'm headed out. I'll be back by suppertime."

He looked at her with his goofy doggie smile.

She ruffled the top of his head. "Be good and guard the cottage."

At those words he trotted to the front door and parked himself, as if he really had understood.

Priscilla laughed as she grabbed her purse and keys. Once she was in the car, she rolled her windows down and let the island breeze blow through the car as she navigated around Vineyard Haven and drove along Beach Road toward Oak Bluffs. As she crossed the bridge she thought of *Jaws* and the shark she'd recovered for a museum last fall. Then she took the road along the shore past the East Chop Lighthouse. It looked similar to her lighthouse as it stood near the water's edge on a spit of sandy, grass-covered land that pushed into the Nantucket Sound. Then it was on into Oak Bluffs. The campground felt like it should be set apart from the community, but in reality Oak Bluffs had grown up around the camp, embracing it inside the town.

She parked at Oak Bluffs Harbor and enjoyed the five-minute walk to the association office. Housed in one of the cottages, it would give her the opportunity to see the inside of another of the unique homes.

The small cottages, painted in an assortment of bright colors, brought a smile to her face. One had an elaborate sign painted with the name *Oz* hanging over the porch. Another had delicate scrollwork that was painted white against a bright blue background. The hot-pink houses made her grin, but her favorites were the rainbow-colored houses, with bright colors taking turns on different features. The elaborate details and attention to upkeep made the area a delight to walk through. The Tabernacle, with its dozens of colored-glass windows and octagonal cupola, anchored the camp as it had since it was erected in 1879.

The cottages looked like life-sized dollhouses, and after exploring Wanda's, Priscilla knew the insides matched the outside. The rooms were small, providing space to relax, but Priscilla imagined many would spend the bulk of their camp time on the porches. Most cottages held porches with chairs perched for the shade. What the porches didn't shade, the trees would, much as they did on large sections of the campgrounds as she walked toward the office.

A few clusters of people were walking around the campground, many with cameras out, capturing the charm. She had to smile as she watched people maneuvering to find the perfect selfie. With so many options, some whirled around as they snapped shots. Because the Cottage Museum was the main way people could see the inside of a cottage, there was a steady stream of people going in and out of the sage-green cottage whose large flag flapped from the porch.

She crossed the street and mounted the stairs to the association office. She rapped on the door, and a few moments later heard someone call for her to come in. She opened the door and entered a small entry space.

A woman dressed in a flowing navy maxi dress and a floral cardigan hurried toward her on wedge sandals from what was probably the small kitchen. "Sorry about that. You should always come right in if the door's unlocked."

"It felt a bit like breaking in."

The forty-something woman laughed and extended her perfectly manicured hand. "I get that. I'm Renee Overman."

"Priscilla Grant. I'm helping Wanda Shire with her cottage."

"So she said." Renee led the way to a small desk and gestured to the chair in front of it. "Have a seat. Now how can I help you?"

Priscilla gave her a quick recap of what they'd found in Wanda's cottage the day before. "What surprised us is that Wanda doesn't remember the ship."

"Sounds big enough to be unforgettable."

"Exactly. My current thought is that one of the guests who rented the cabin over the last year may have left it."

Renee frowned but turned to wiggle the mouse and wake up her computer. "If the ship's that big, I'm not sure it's an item some-one could forget. It's not like a rubber ball that rolls under a bed, but Wanda said to help you. I had to call her to get her permission, you know."

"Of course. And I agree with you. Originally I thought the ship had been wrapped up and tucked down in the bottom drawer for safekeeping and then forgotten. But if that were so, Wanda should still remember it when it resurfaced. She didn't."

"What does it look like?"

Priscilla pulled out her phone and showed Renee a couple of the photos.

Renee's red lips formed a perfect *O*. "Wow, that's quite a find." She turned back to her computer. "When do you want to start looking?"

"The last two years' rentals if possible."

"Well." Renee clicked a few buttons, but lines had appeared along her forehead as she avoided looking at Priscilla. "It makes me nervous to give you all that information."

"How many people rent the cottage in a typical summer?"

"Rentals are supposed to be for a week, though Wanda is willing to make the occasional exception. I'd say it's usually about thirteen groups."

"Groups?"

"Yes. One week that might be a family, the next week old friends, the week after that a couple of college buddies. The cottages aren't big enough to host large groups, but you'd be amazed how many can cram in when they're motivated." She shook her head. "One time there must have been a sleeping bag covering every free inch. It looked like an unending stream of people in and out."

"I hope it wasn't too much to clean."

"That was the ironic thing. By the time they left it almost looked like no one had stayed there." Renee chewed her lower lip a minute. Then she nodded. "I'll give you a list of last year's guests and a contact number and email address for each. If you can't find someone who knows the ship from that list, then we'll go back another year."

"I can work with that."

"We don't tell people we'll release their information to third parties."

"I won't use it for any other purpose than to find the owner of the ship."

"I understand that, but I'm not sure they will." Her hands hovered over the keyboard. "I suppose, since I talked to Wanda, I can assure them, if any of them complain, that you are acting as her agent. Just give me a minute and I'll print out the list."

"Thank you." Priscilla picked up a brochure and flipped through it while Renee clicked away on her keyboard. Several of the brochure's pictures highlighted the tabernacle along with select cottages in sherbet colors. Then on the next page there were profiles of several owners with information about how they became part of the campground community. The walls of the office were covered with a series of photos highlighting events around the grounds.

"Looks like you have lots of activities here." More than Priscilla had been aware of.

"Yes. We'll be hopping from this weekend through Labor Day."

The printer started whirring, and a moment later Renee handed Priscilla a sheet of paper with the list. "This should have everything you need to contact the guests."

Priscilla accepted the list with thanks, then glanced over it. None of the names were familiar to her, but she didn't expect to recognize those who'd been on the island for only a week. "Are any of these people return guests? Regulars who like to come back every year?"

Renee frowned as she considered the question. "There are three who have come back more than once that I remember. But I've only worked here for five years, so it's possible that others are returning after a longer stretch of time."

"I see. If they have that many years between visits, it's not likely they're the ones who left the ship. It wouldn't take years for someone to find it."

Priscilla folded the sheet of paper and tucked it into her purse. "Thanks for your time. If all goes well, I won't have to bother you again."

"No problem." Renee stood and held out her hand again. "Wanda is an important client, and I'm happy to help her in any way I can."

Priscilla stood and shook Renee's hand. "One last question." At Renee's arched brow, Priscilla laughed and then backpedaled. "I guess I shouldn't promise it's the last one. How does managing the cabins work? Do you manage all of them?"

"No, we don't. All the owners pay an association fee each year for grounds maintenance, etc. But many handle renting the cottages out themselves or use another company. Wanda asked me to help her, and I was happy to do so."

"Why did she ask you?"

"Because I also own a cottage here, and it's always rented. Usually has a waiting list too, and Wanda wanted that for her cottage. Maintaining a cottage isn't inexpensive, especially as the grounds age. Those costs have to be recouped somewhere, and when she was wrestling with keeping or selling the cottage, she asked if I would try managing it for a year." She smiled and shrugged. "I guess you could say I was successful."

"So how many years have you managed the cottage for Wanda?"

"The last four. And she's kept the cottage in the family. That's the key."

Priscilla could see how that would be important. "And it's worth your time?"

"Yes." Pink stole up her neck, and she looked away. "I get ten percent of the rental fee. But I also coordinate the cleaning and maintenance when it needs it."

Priscilla nodded. "I'm sure that's a help to Wanda." She hitched her purse on her shoulder and smiled. "Thank you again for your time and help. And for answering my extra questions."

"Good luck." The phone rang, and Renee answered it as Priscilla headed out the door.

There was little activity on the green as she walked down the cottage steps. It looked like a few people were taking the self-tour, and one carload was checking in to a cottage. As she walked to the harbor where her car was parked, she noticed the plants that were beginning to bud. In a few weeks the grounds would explode with late-spring blooms as the area waltzed into early summer. The campground would be an even more beautiful walk then.

Priscilla tapped the side of her purse and felt for the printout Renee had given her. She pulled it out and unfolded it. With the quick glance she'd given it at the association office, she hadn't noticed any names she recognized. Now she had the time and space to examine the list in more detail. Regina Farmer. David Scott. Owen Landers. The list continued without a name that she could identify. She put the list back in her purse and quickened her steps. She was excited to get home and get started. She felt sure she'd have her answers in another hour or so. How hard could it be?

CHAPTER EIGHT

Two hours and fourteen voice mails later, Priscilla was no longer excited.

The moment she'd gotten home, she'd put the list on the kitchen table along with a pad and pen. After fixing a mug of coffee, she'd settled on the bistro chair and pulled the list closer.

She reached for her phone and dialed the first number. The call went to voice mail. So did the next one. She left a message for each call, explaining who she was and what she'd found and asking them to call back. By the time she'd reached the fourteenth name and hadn't talked to a living soul, she'd begun to wonder if her own caller ID showed up on people's screens as "Don't Waste Your Time."

She knew many people didn't pick up calls from numbers they didn't recognize, but it seemed odd that *no one* had answered. She turned to her computer. Maybe an email would open the door and someone would call her back.

She quickly typed up a basic message.

Hello, my name is Priscilla Grant. I am helping Wanda Shire identify the owner of an item we found in her cottage at the Martha's Vineyard Camp Meeting Association. Her records indicate that you rented the cottage located at 29 Clinton Way last year.

We recently discovered a three-foot metal replica of a ship in one of the bedrooms. Because it isn't Wanda's she asked me to contact you to see if it might be yours. If you think it might be yours or to learn more, please call me at the following number.

Then she listed her number. She wondered about attaching a photo of the ship, but decided to leave that for those who requested an image.

She entered the first email address into the recipient's box, and then added the other addresses as blind copies. She hit Send. All fourteen renters would find an email waiting in their in-boxes.

Now what?

She switched to a search engine and entered the first name on the list in the search box. Regina Farmer didn't pull up many results, but as she scanned them, Priscilla realized it would be almost impossible to know which was the right Regina. And that was assuming the search located her.

Then she entered the next name: David Scott. But even as she typed she knew it would be too common for anything helpful to come up. One look at the number of search results told her she was right.

She leaned back against the chair's back and considered her options. She could give the emails a little bit of time to be received and read or she could start calling again.

When her phone rang, she welcomed the interruption.

"Hello, Joan."

"Priscilla." Joan's voice was warm and teasing. This cousin had become a close friend since Priscilla had moved to the island. "I hear you've been planting ideas in Gail's mind."

"About *American Antiques*?"

Her cousin's laughter was rich. "No, no. About Uncle Hugh. I know you're in matchmaking mode."

"Hugh's already engaged. There's no match to be made."

"Okay, okay. But that's not why I'm calling. Trudy and I were bored and thought it was a good evening for a cousin supper. Want to join us at my house? It'll be simple, but the company will be good."

That it would. Priscilla loved that her move to Martha's Vineyard had resulted in warm resurrected relationships with her cousins. The time would also keep her from focusing too much on uncovering the ship's secrets. "I don't have anything pressing to do tonight."

"Then why don't you come over about seven? We'll have something light to eat, and then we can hang out on the porch."

"Or play games." Trudy's voice trickled into Priscilla's ear from the background.

"Does that mean Dan is gone on a research trip?"

"For the weekend, and Trudy needs to be entertained."

"Hey. I am not needy."

Priscilla laughed even as she shook her head at the teasing between her cousins. "I'll see you then. And I'll bring something sweet."

"Well, I've already made my famous bread pudding."

At that sentence, Priscilla's mouth started watering. Joan had won a national bake-off award years earlier, and even though she allowed several local restaurants to use her recipe, they could never get it to turn out quite like hers. Priscilla had even asked her if she had a secret ingredient, but Joan had demurred. "Then I will gladly eat my share. See you soon."

A few minutes before seven Priscilla pulled into the driveway of her cousin's cottage. Joan's English-inspired gardens were beginning to show life and a hint of what they would be at the height of summer. The plants didn't block the view of the ocean yet, but by the end of May the trellises would barely be visible. In any season of the year, Joan's gardens were some of the prettiest on the island, whether covered by a blanket of snow or a carpet of flowers. And having the Atlantic Ocean as a backdrop certainly didn't hurt.

Trudy and Joan were sitting on the small porch when Priscilla walked up. Another car pulled up behind her, and Gail got out. Joan welcomed both of them with a quiet smile, while Trudy stood and threw her arms around her cousins. Joan and Trudy were so different, yet similar in a way that only happened with sisters. Joan's dog, Sister, nestled next to her owner, but her ear's pricked up in Priscilla's direction.

"I'm amazed at how well Sister is doing, Joan." The early days and weeks hadn't been easy for Joan as she'd adjusted to life with a rambunctious puppy. To her credit, Joan had stuck with it, doing the hard work of training a dog.

"All that time and those classes were worth it."

Trudy winked at Priscilla. "You didn't see her bribe Sister with her favorite treat. She won't move a muscle if it means she gets a dental stick."

Joan rolled her eyes. "We do what we must."

"Ah, the royal we." Trudy moved toward the front door. "I'm glad you could come. The house was way too lonely to stay there by myself."

Trudy had a gorgeous two-story home, one that reflected her hospitable nature. Whereas Joan had invested her time in creating beautiful, restful gardens, Trudy had a knack for creating spaces that invited a person to step inside and release the day's cares. More than once, Priscilla had experienced that grace in the right moment.

Priscilla noticed the basket over Gail's arm. "What have you got in there?"

"Fresh biscuits. Dad wanted biscuits and gravy for supper, so I brought the extra biscuits here. I've wrapped them well, so they should still be warm."

"Those will go great with the ham." Joan led everyone into her cottage, her small, quick steps reminding Priscilla of a sparrow. With Joan's small build and short brown hair, the image fit her well.

Also petite, Trudy followed a step behind. Her platinum-blonde hair was pulled back in a low ponytail. Her wedge sandals slapped against the floor with a staccato burst.

"Can you make those shoes a little louder?" Gail winked at Priscilla. "I can almost hear myself think."

"You're just jealous because they're stylish." Trudy kicked a foot forward to show off the shoe in question.

"Yep, jealous that I could break my neck in those." Gail linked arms with Priscilla, and they walked to Joan's kitchen. "It smells really good, Joan."

The scent of something salty and sweet filled the air.

"It's just ham with pineapple. The real reason we're here is my bread pudding, so I didn't want to distract from that." She pulled a plate filled with ham and then a warming pan of green beans with slivered almonds to the front of her stove. Gail set the basket of biscuits next to it. "We can fill our plates here and then eat at the table on the patio."

In short order the plates were filled, and each cousin had grabbed a glass of tea with fresh mint sprigs. After a quick blessing, they dug into the food. Priscilla enjoyed the companionship and the setting for the meal.

"This was a wonderful idea, Joan." Priscilla buttered her biscuit. "We should consider making evenings like this a regular thing."

"It might lose the spontaneity." Trudy dabbed the corners of her mouth with a napkin before replacing it in her lap.

"But then we wouldn't have to work to get together." Gail speared another piece of ham. "Because you know, it is work."

"It's something to consider." Joan pushed to her feet. "Anyone else need anything? More tea?"

There was a chorus of no-thank-yous, so she returned to the patio after a few minutes with four bowls of bread pudding. Priscilla let each bite linger in her mouth, just as she let her mind linger in the moment. She hadn't realized just how much she needed this easygoing back-and-forth when she moved to the island.

Trudy scraped her plate with her fork. "If you'll make me bread pudding every time Dan leaves, I might have to urge an overnight trip for him a few more times a year."

Joan snorted as she laughed. "That's terrible. All you have to do is ask." She turned to Priscilla. "Gail told me a bit about your ship. Any luck with it?"

"Not yet. I left a lot of voice mails and sent a round of emails. Your call was perfectly timed to keep me from compulsively calling everyone again." She spread her hands on the table. "You'd think I have a vested interest in the ship."

Trudy propped her elbows on the table and leaned in. "Why are you searching for the owner?"

"Because Wanda needs the help, and I'm curious. We need to know if it's worth taking to *American Antiques*. Besides, Gail asked for my help. That's reason enough."

Gail reached over and took her hand. "Thank you. I'd like to go back to the cottage tomorrow and look around."

"I don't know what we'll find. It seems like we looked thoroughly, but I'll try to go with you, if you like. We can go right after church, then I'm having dinner with Gerald. I'm hoping he'll have something to tell me about the ship."

Joan pulled out a set of dominoes and they played a rousing game of chicken foot. The best part was the light and easy conversation that flowed as the dominoes clicked and the lines grew. Nothing could make Priscilla's heart fuller than it was as she drove home.

As she entered her cottage and saw the ship waiting, the warm feeling from the evening followed her. She let Jake out to do his business, then got ready for bed. Gerald called just as she was turning out the lights in the living room.

"Hey you." Priscilla kicked off her slippers and climbed under her covers.

"Hey yourself," Gerald said. "How was the get-together at Joan's house?"

"We're all filled up with bread pudding. Don't worry—I saved you some. It's in my refrigerator as we speak." She laughed.

"Good to know. I'll claim it tomorrow after we go to dinner. Want to go to the Nautilus?"

"That depends. Will the maritime theme inspire you to tell me about the ship?"

Gerald chuckled. "I think that can be arranged. I don't know everything I want to know about it, but I can tell you generally what it is."

"Are you sure you don't want to tell me now?" she teased. "You'd sleep a lot better, getting it off your chest."

His voice softened. "I'll sleep a lot better knowing I'm going to be looking into your eyes tomorrow."

Priscilla's heart melted. Ship? What ship?

CHAPTER NINE

Sunday morning, Priscilla lay in bed a little longer than usual, enjoying a few minutes to collect her thoughts. Sunlight filtered into her room, coloring it with light, and Jake came up and pressed his nose into her hand. He nudged, and she groaned but got up. She pulled her robe on and walked to the front of the house to let him out. The ship sat on the coffee table where she had left it, a reminder that there were puzzles she hadn't solved yet. She checked her phone, but no return messages waited.

She'd decided that, after she and Gail went back to the cottage, she'd check email and see if anyone had responded.

When Jake was ready to come back inside she remembered Gerald's words from Friday. Maybe she should look around her cottage and the lighthouse for anything that could be worth taking to the show. It would be interesting to learn the story behind something that had become familiar and maybe invisible to her in the time she'd been on the island.

Maybe she had a hidden treasure sitting unnoticed on a wall or resting on a shelf. The thought was an intriguing one.

It gave her fresh eyes as she prepared breakfast and dressed for church. Could there be unseen value in her old-fashioned coffee-pot? What about the lace table runner she'd laid along the top of a dresser? Was it worn because it was old or because it had been overused without care? All she knew was she loved the delicate filigree pattern and the ivory color.

Many items around the cottage generated similar responses. This was home. Every inch of the small, four-room cottage. It was filled with details that made each day a homecoming and filled her with peace when she walked in the door. That was a gift she'd hoped for when she moved to Martha's Vineyard.

An hour later, she was at church, ready to worship with her friends. The Sunday school hour in the fellowship hall was filled with her favorite people. Ida Lee Jones had stopped at Candy Lane Confectionery Saturday and picked up scones for the class. Priscilla selected a blueberry-lemon one and let the flaky treat melt in her mouth before chasing it down with coffee.

Gerald arrived a few minutes after ten, which was unusual for the man who usually ran on military precision. He grabbed a cup of black coffee and claimed the chair next to Priscilla. "How's my girl?"

She turned toward him, a hand at her throat as if that could hide the pleasure his words brought her. "I've decided to look around my cottage later today for potential items to take to *American Antiques*."

"Wonderful. I think you'll find a gem or two. I haven't forgotten I'm going to look through the lighthouse for you."

"I don't know if I'll find anything, but this morning I woke up wondering what might be lying around me that I don't even notice anymore. It's fun to imagine what could be lurking right under my nose."

"The treasures."

"Exactly." She shrugged and took another sip of coffee. "It could all be trash to someone else, but it's an interesting exercise to consider what might have value."

As the study time started, Priscilla felt the warmth of the man sitting next to her and the friendship of the others surrounding her. This was home, and she loved the people and this church. Then the service filled her cup with the combination of worship time and a sermon that challenged her to consider her life practically. At the conclusion, she shook hands with Curt Lannister, the new pastor. He'd made the transition from his church of urban professionals, and it looked like his family was settling in as well. Priscilla noticed he'd worn khakis and a polo instead of the suit he'd worn when he first arrived. Even his wife, Clarissa, had started to settle into the relaxed island style while retaining flashes of urban chic.

"Thank you for another insightful sermon, Pastor Curt."

His grin was a tad sheepish. "I hope you aren't just trying to be nice."

"Stick around awhile, and you'll see I usually say what I mean." She turned to Clarissa, who had stepped up to join her husband. "Are you feeling settled?"

"Down to a row of boxes in the garage, and we have most of the wall hangings up, so it feels like our place." Clarissa smiled, revealing perfect teeth that had a spot of lipstick on one. "We already love it here."

"Wait until the tourists arrive later this month. It changes the energy on the island for the season."

Pastor Curt took his wife's hand. "We're looking forward to experiencing that part of island living."

"If you need anything, just call." Priscilla headed outside to her car and saw Gerald leaning against it.

"I didn't want to interrupt your conversation with Pastor Curt."

"Ah. Do you want to come look in the lighthouse now?"

"If you have time."

"I do until Gail calls me. She and Uncle Hugh go to the late service." Priscilla hiked her purse higher on her shoulder. "We're supposed to go back to the campground today."

"Why?"

Priscilla caught him up to speed on the ship. "We visited Wanda yesterday, and she says she's never seen the ship. That led me to trying to track down who could have left it."

Gerald raised his eyebrows as he watched her. "How are you doing that?"

"I've got the list of renters from last year and am trying to reach all of them. Emphasis on *trying*. So far no luck, and that's after calling and emailing each one."

He opened her car door for her. "Let's go see what you have."

Gerald followed her to her house. She glanced in the rearview mirror at a stoplight, and Gerald waved. She raised her hand and waved her fingers in response. A few minutes later they were out of Vineyard Haven and on the road to her cottage. He pulled into the lighthouse's driveway behind her and somehow managed to get to her car door before she'd had time to open it.

He held out his hand with a gallant half bow. "May I be of assistance, madam?"

She grinned up at him. "Why, thank you, kind sir."

A moment later she walked to her front door with him at her side.

She set her purse on the small table by the door and hung her keys on their hook. "If you'll give me a minute, I'll get us some iced tea."

Tea glasses in hand, they walked through the living room, studying the items scattered around.

Priscilla watched as Gerald scanned the area. "What are you looking for?"

"I'm not really sure. Can I say I'll know it when I see it?"

She laughed. "Sure."

He picked up the porcelain swan that sat on one of the shelves. "Maybe something like this?"

She took the swan from him. "While I agree it's pretty, I highly doubt something I got at a garage sale for fifty cents will be worth anything."

Gerald grinned. "Maybe you have a Jackson Pollock painting sitting around."

"The abstract artist? I'd recognize that. I do have some culture, you know."

"A lady bought one of his paintings at a garage sale for five dollars. You could call that the best five-dollar investment of her life."

"I'd say. I imagine she'd be able to sell it for much more."

"I've heard around nine million."

Priscilla's eyebrows shot up. "I'm pretty certain there's nothing like that lurking in a corner here, though it would be nice." She paused as her gaze landed on the ship. "Unless it's that ship." She clasped her hands and tucked them under her chin. "Speaking of that ship..."

Gerald held his hand up. "You can beg all you want. I'm not saying a word until we sit down to dinner. That was the deal." He grinned. "Although, I have to say, you're pretty cute when you beg."

Priscilla threw her hands up. "You are the most stubborn man on the planet, you know that?"

"It's possible." He turned to the front door. "Want to check the lighthouse with me?"

An hour later she'd forgiven him for being stubborn as he wove elaborate tales about the backgrounds of many of the items. According to him one compass had been used by Bluebeard himself. While it was fascinating and kept her in stitches, she didn't find anything to take to the show.

After he left, she decided it was a good time to check her email.

Just as she sat down at her computer hoping to find some answers, her phone rang.

CHAPTER TEN

Gail's voice came rattling through the phone at about three hundred words a minute.

"Take a breath, Gail." Priscilla paused as if to demonstrate. "What happened? Is there an emergency? Is your dad okay?"

Gail inhaled and then blew out the breath. "Sorry. It's been one of those days."

"On a Sunday?"

"Just shenanigans between the churches." Grace Community, where Gail attended, had an ongoing, mostly friendly rivalry with Wesley Chapel. They shared a fence and an interesting dynamic. "Someone put flyers for a Wesley event on all our cars."

"Was it to a membership class?"

"What?" Gail sputtered to a stop. "No. It was a flyer about their Vacation Bible School."

"It's not the same week as your VBS, is it?"

"Well, no." Gail took another deep breath and released it slowly. "I guess I overreacted. Dad's been on a tear, and it's got me on edge."

"Anything I can do?"

"Other than move him out?" She chuckled wryly. "No. Now to the real reason I called. Ready to head to Wanda's?"

"Want me to meet you there?"

"No, I can be by in forty-five minutes."

"That gives me time to take Jake for a quick walk, so he'll be grateful."

"See you soon."

By the time Gail arrived at the cottage, she seemed to have shed her earlier stress. She smiled as Priscilla climbed into the car. "Well, they've made a decision."

Priscilla closed her door and pulled on her seat belt. "Who has?"

"Dad and Marigold. They want a small ceremony at the lighthouse, if you're really willing."

"Absolutely. When?"

"Does the Sunday before Memorial Day work?"

That would give them a week to get the details in place. "It should work well if they truly want simple. What do you need from me?"

"The primary thing right now is knowing that we can use the lighthouse grounds."

"Absolutely. Let me know if you need anything else. I have a few contacts around for tables and chairs and catering."

"Thanks. It sounds like simple is better as far as they're concerned, and that definitely helps." Gail's shoulders relaxed, and Priscilla was glad to watch the transformation in her friend. "So did you have any luck with the renters?"

"Not yet. I'm actually surprised I haven't heard back from any of them. I have to remind myself it was only last night that I left that round of messages and emails."

"I'd guess you'll start hearing from them Monday. Unless the ship doesn't belong to any of them. Besides, any email address my computer doesn't recognize goes straight to junk mail, and I don't check it very regularly. And if I get a call I don't recognize, I wait to listen to the voice mail."

"True. Though I thought someone would be curious enough to contact me." She shrugged as they drove along Beach Road. If she focused, the peace of the narrow beach and the soothing waves could wash over her. "It's funny how vested I am in finding out where that ship came from."

"I'll be honest. My only goal is to find something to take to the show that will wow the hosts. It means so much to Wanda, and with her trapped in that wheelchair, it seems like a way to brighten this season for her." Gail grinned as she slowed behind a car that was taking its time, likely filled with tourists who wanted to capture every breathtaking view. "It would be incredible to be the one who showed up with the item Tim and Cherish gush over."

"And if it's valuable..."

"All the better."

Priscilla laughed. "Gerald came over after church to help me find something to take."

"Did you?"

"No, but he enjoyed looking."

The silence that settled in the car was broken only by the cries of seagulls as they soared out over the water and then flew back to settle on the sand. Several were engaged in a stiff-legged dance along the edge of the water where it kissed the sand. Gail turned away from the shore and onto County Road for the drive into Oak Bluffs and the Martha's Vineyard Camp Meeting Association. Soon she'd parked at the harbor, and they walked to the campgrounds.

A few more people strolled the grounds, many with camera or phone at the ready. Their delight in the miniature sherbet-colored Victorian cottages was evident.

Gail led the way to Wanda's cottage and, once she had unlocked the door, they stepped inside. The cottage was shadowed in darkness, so Priscilla opened the drapes.

Her phone buzzed in her purse, and she pulled it from the depths of the bag. The number wasn't one she recognized. Could it be someone returning her call from the prior day? She took the call with a quick hello as she set her purse on the floor.

"Hi, this is Luke Brainerd. You called me about the ship you found?"

"Thanks for calling, Luke. It's my understanding you stayed at a cottage on Clinton Avenue in the Martha's Vineyard Camp Association last year."

"Yeah, stayed there in August, right before school started. It was charming, but I think my wife liked it more than I did."

"Oh?"

"The rooms were a little small for me, but if she liked it, that's what matters."

Priscilla chuckled at his boisterous enthusiasm. "Sounds like she had a great time."

"So what did you need to know? Your message was kind of garbled."

"Sorry about that." Priscilla sank onto one of the beds and felt the warmth of the sun streaming through the narrow window. A child ran along the sidewalk, delight on her face as she led a dog on a leash. "I'm helping a friend who owns the cottage you stayed in. Friday we found a ship that isn't hers tucked in a drawer, and I'm trying to help her find the owner."

"Huh."

She waited a moment, but when he didn't say anything more, she continued. "Could you have left anything behind?"

"I'm pretty sure we would have noticed by now. It's been what, nine months?"

"All right. Well, thank you for your time."

"No problem. Good luck with your search."

When the call ended, Priscilla tapped the phone against her chin and headed into the hall. That call hadn't told her much. "Gail, what do you know about Renee Overman?"

Gail looked up from her phone. "I know of her, but haven't really spent time with her. Why?"

Priscilla couldn't quite identify what was bothering her, but something about the way Renee had been hesitant to help didn't sit right. They headed upstairs. "Wanda talked to Renee before I came over right?"

"That's what she said."

"Then she should have been willing to help me, but she wasn't. I had to talk her into giving me the names." She didn't like the direction her thoughts were headed, but Gail was a good one to talk through the puzzle with. "What if she doesn't want me to talk to the renters?"

"Wanda? Or Renee?"

"I'm not sure." As she admitted that, she felt foolish. "Never mind. I'm just disappointed that it's taking so long to find a clue to this puzzle."

Now that she knew the ship wasn't supposed to be here, she could look through the bedroom for any indication of who might have left it. That was different than Friday's search for interesting items. When she entered the bedroom she headed to the dresser and opened the bottom drawer. It slid open easily, and when she stared in the drawer, there was nothing inside.

CHAPTER ELEVEN

Where were the toys?

She'd put them back in the drawer before leaving Friday afternoon.

She stood and went to the stairs. "Gail?"

"Yes?" Her cousin came to stand at the bottom of the stairs.

"Do you remember what I did with the wooden toys that were in the twin bedroom?"

"I thought you replaced them in the drawer."

Priscilla nodded, but her shoulders tightened, and she must have made a face because Gail started up the stairs.

"What's wrong?"

"The toys are gone."

"What? They should be right there."

"I know." Priscilla rubbed her forehead and tried to think where else they could be. She went back into the bedroom and opened the other drawers in the dresser. The toys hadn't been slipped into one of them. She checked under each bed. Still nothing.

Gail reached the top of the stairs. "I'll check the other bedroom."

"Thanks." Priscilla paused and turned a slow circle in the middle of the room. Something was bothering her, but she couldn't put her finger on it. What was different?

After a minute, Gail came and stood in the doorway. "Nothing seems different about that bedroom." She cocked her head as she watched Priscilla. "What's wrong?"

"What do you mean?"

"I know you well enough to know you're unsettled."

That was the wonderful and scary part about being with her cousin. They really did know each other well enough to make those kinds of determinations. "Those toys didn't wander away on their own."

"No, but we'll find them."

Could the toys have value? Had she missed the fact that maybe they weren't just common wooden toys?

As Gail locked up the cottage, Priscilla noted that the association office looked closed. She'd have to wait until tomorrow to ask Renee if anyone had been in the cabin since Friday.

After a quick bite at a fast-food place, Gail dropped Priscilla off at home. She checked her computer for emails—none—and spent the rest of the afternoon and early evening playing with Jake, catching up on some reading, and trying not to think about model ships. Gerald came by about seven to take her to dinner. As they rode to the Nautilus Café they chitchatted about how his inspection had gone the day before, and she caught him up on the latest in the Wanda saga—the missing toys.

When they'd been seated and ordered their entrées, Gerald took her hand and squeezed it. "I think what I've discovered will be of great interest to you, Priscilla." He leaned back in his chair. "Both as a lighthouse owner, and as the particular 'friend'"—he grinned—"of a Coast Guard captain."

Priscilla raised her eyebrows, intrigued. "As a lighthouse owner?"

"Hmm..." Gerald looked disappointed. "Nothing to say about the 'friend' comment?"

Priscilla laughed. "You'll be my very best friend in the whole entire world if you'll tell me what I've been waiting forty-eight hours to hear."

"I'll take that," Gerald said. He paused dramatically. "Your model ship is a Coast Guard lightship."

"What?" Priscilla exclaimed. "What is a lightship?"

"They're essentially floating lighthouses, used to warn mariners of rocks and shoals during reduced visibility. They were first used in the early 1700s, in England, and then in America in the early 1800s. Right around the time the Second World War began, the Coast Guard assumed command over the country's lightships."

Priscilla clasped her hands together. "Gerald, how wonderful! So you thought it might be that when you first saw it?"

Gerald nodded. "I did. But I wanted to make sure, because I knew how much it would mean to you."

"Well, it's a delightful surprise. I wonder if we'll ever know if the lightship is a generic one, or if it was a particular one." Priscilla took a sip of her water. "I guess there's no way to know."

"I can't think of any way we could find that out," agreed Gerald. "We certainly can't read the name on the side anymore."

Priscilla took his hand. "Well, it's enough for me to know it's a Coast Guard lightship. I really appreciate you finding that out. It's almost like I was meant to find it."

The waiter brought their entrées, and the rest of the meal was spent talking about Gerald's grandchildren and Rachel's upcoming wedding. Because Gerald had an early day the next morning, they skipped dessert and he drove her home.

They held hands as they walked to the door. Gerald gave her a gentle hug and kiss before letting her go, and Priscilla sighed with contentment. "Call me when you get home?"

He kissed the tip of her nose. "Count on it."

Priscilla floated into the house, her thoughts not quite entirely on a certain model ship.

She'd settled on her couch with a mug of hot tea and her laptop when her phone rang. She grabbed it from the end table.

"Is this Mrs. Grant?"

"It is."

"Hello, I'm Nathan Radford. You left a message about the cabin we rented last fall."

Priscilla frowned as she scrambled to grab the sheet Renee had given her with guests. "Last fall?"

"Yeah, we rented it for a long weekend in September."

"I had you as renting it in June."

He laughed. "Nope. We were still living in California then. My employer relocated us to the East Coast in July, and we're trying to see all this side of the country has to offer before he moves us again. He's got me on the fast track to working in all the corporate locations."

Priscilla scanned the list and confirmed that it had all the dates from the window of Memorial Day to Labor Day. Maybe the dates had been flipped, and the group that rented it for Labor Day were really earlier in the season. "Did you enjoy the stay?"

"Sure did. We commented when we left how glad we were to grab that weekend. My wife had heard about the campground from family members, and the Relic was even better than we'd hoped. We were lucky to snag those days because another group cancelled the first four days of their stay, and we were top of the waiting list."

Priscilla's frown deepened. "Our records got confused somewhere along the way. Could you tell me which dates you stayed?"

"Sure. It was September 21 to 24."

"What a great time to be here. The fall colors are gorgeous then."

"They sure were."

"Did you happen to see the ship I mentioned in my voice mail? It's about three feet long and was wrapped in a cloth."

"Is that what's missing? Sorry, but we didn't take it."

"Actually, it appeared."

"Huh." He paused. "We didn't leave it."

"Oh well." Priscilla glanced at the ship where it rested on the coffee table. "Thanks for calling me back, and welcome to the East Coast."

After she hung up she sat staring at the ship, then at the list.

Why would the Radfords' time at the cottage be mislabeled by months? June 21st was three months earlier. Was it a simple clerical error? She added the question to the growing list for Renee.

The next morning, after taking Jake on his walk, Priscilla was hanging up his leash when she heard Gerald's ringtone. She worked her phone out of her pocket and smiled at his handsome face on the screen before answering the call. "Hey, you. Was there something you forgot to tell me last night?"

He laughed. "Hey yourself. Well, let's see. Did I tell you I love you?"

She got goose bumps. "Yes, actually, you did. Twice."

"Then, nope. I didn't forget anything. I'm calling to tell you I found out this morning I have to go out of town for a couple of days. I've been assigned to an inspection at the Provincetown station. Chickie and I are leaving in a couple of hours."

"How long will you be gone?"

"I should be back on Wednesday sometime, hopefully before noon. I was wondering something…"

"What's that?"

"Would it be all right if I took the ship with me to Provincetown? There might be someone there who could tell us more about it."

"I think that's a great idea. Do you have time to come get it, or should I bring it to you?"

"Chickie said he could swing by there on his way. He'll be there in about thirty minutes, if that's okay with you."

"Sure. That'll work. Call me tonight?"

"Count on it."

Priscilla hung up and searched her closets for a suitable box to pack the model ship in. She found a large plastic tub with a lid and dragged it into the living room. She lined the tub with an old quilt and placed the ship inside, then filled the empty spaces around it with some old towels. Jake sat quietly and watched her every move.

She sat back on her heels. A lightship. She pictured the ship on a stormy winter's night, anchored offshore near a rocky shoal, its light the only warning a seafaring vessel would have of impending danger. She saw the crew battling the blizzard, fighting to get to the lamps to keep the beacons shining across the waves that crashed against the ship. What was it inside these brave men that drove them to endure such punishment for others?

She was startled out of her reverie by the sound of a car horn. She sighed. "It would be nice if you could simply tell me where you came from."

Jake cocked his head.

"Yes, I am well aware I just talked to an inanimate object." She laid another quilt on top of the ship and put the lid on. "Wouldn't it be ironic if I'm spending all this time on something that's only worth forty dollars?"

While Chickie carried the box to his vehicle, she quickly wrapped up the two pieces of bread pudding she should have given Gerald last night and gave them to Chickie for the trip to Provincetown. It was a lot easier to remember things like bread pudding when a handsome Coast Guard captain wasn't gazing into your eyes and pulling you close.

She waved goodbye to Chickie, made sure Jake was settled, and drove back to the campground. She'd stopped at Candy's on her way for two to-go cups of coffee and a couple of scones. It was a peace offering of sorts to hopefully ease Renee toward openness as Priscilla asked hard questions. She sank onto the front steps of the association's office and enjoyed the spring sunshine warming her face as she waited for Renee.

Renee was easy to see from a distance. She wore a fuchsia cardigan over a colorfully striped maxi dress. Her outfit looked like a box of markers had exploded on the fabric creating a kaleidoscope effect. Her wedge sandals' straps were each a different color too. Her steps faltered when she spotted Priscilla.

"Did we have an appointment?" Her tone was cautious.

"Sorry, I had a couple of quick questions and thought it would be easier to ask them in person rather than over the phone. I grabbed coffee and scones. Do you like coffee?" Priscilla held up the cups. "I have a latte or a cappuccino."

"The latte would be great, thank you. Well, come on in." Renee walked around Priscilla and up the stairs. She unlocked the door, and Priscilla followed her into the office. She set her purse and keys on the desk, then leaned against the desk and looked at Priscilla. "So how can I help?"

"I've talked to a couple of the guests." Priscilla handed her the latte. "Here's a sugar packet if you need it."

"Thanks." She set the sugar packet on the desk, then took a sip of the drink.

"When I talked with Nathan Radford, he said they stayed at Wanda's cottage in September."

Renee shrugged. "It's possible. So?"

"The list you gave me has him renting it in June."

"I must have entered it wrong, or he made a mistake. It happens."

Priscilla watched her, not buying the easy answer. "I don't think so, because if you put people in the wrong slots, then you risk double-booking the cabin."

"So it got changed by mistake after the fact. I had an intern who wasn't great at details. That's likely when it happened." Renee looked unconcerned, but the excuse felt contrived to Priscilla.

"He also mentioned there was someone who stayed in the cottage after them."

"Like I told you Saturday, it's usually booked through the season."

"When does the season usually end?"

Renee frowned at her. "You live here. You should know the answer to that."

"But I don't know the season from the hospitality side." She didn't manage the occasional groups that came to the lighthouse or make her living from the tourists. She was happy to leave that to others.

"The high season ends at Labor Day, and the shoulder season peters out by Columbus Day." She sounded bored. Priscilla suspected Renee would probably smack her gum in indifference if she were chewing any.

"So who stayed in the cottage after the high season ended?"

"Nobody. Why?"

"Nathan Radford told me they squeezed in four days between other guests, and they were here September 21 through 24. The list you gave me doesn't have anyone staying after Labor Day."

"Well, he's lying. Look, I have a lot to do today. Do you need anything else?"

"Could I have a fresh printout, one that has the Radfords' reservation in the right window?"

"If that means I can start working, sure." She flounced around her desk and powered up her computer. "Did you say you have a scone for me?"

"I do." Priscilla slid the bag across the desk toward Renee. "There's a maple one and a cranberry orange. Take your pick."

Renee picked up the maple scone, clicked some keys, and then frowned as she clicked a few more. The printer whirred to life on the hutch behind her desk. She turned around and grabbed a sheet of paper as it curled off the machine. "Here you go."

"Thanks." Priscilla began to scan it, but Renee cleared her throat. Priscilla looked up and gave what she hoped was a disarming smile. "I'll call if I have other questions."

"I'm sure you will." Renee turned away from her and pointedly focused on her computer.

Priscilla left the office determined to head back to Wanda's cottage. Before she did, though, she needed a plan. She walked across the street and down to the Relic's porch, where she sank onto one of its rocking chairs and ran through the list again. The Radfords' date had moved, but there was no way to know whether any of the other information was accurate. Maybe Wanda could shed some light on the veracity of the information. If nothing else, they could compare any information Wanda had with what Renee had given Priscilla.

Priscilla texted Gail. *Can I get Wanda's phone number from you?*
Sure. Why?
I need to follow up with her on who stayed in the cottage.

Gail sent her the number, and Priscilla called it. A minute later
she had an appointment to see Wanda at her house in two hours.
She decided to use the extra time to touch base with Mildred
Pearson, her friend who ran the East Shore Historical Museum.
The museum sat on the edge of Vineyard Haven, and it took
time to drive from Oak Bluffs to the sunny yellow Queen Anne
Victorian that seemed to smile a welcome each time Priscilla drove
into the small parking lot. She parked next to Mildred's crossover
and hurried to the front door.

When Priscilla entered the museum, she glanced around but
didn't immediately spot Mildred. Her friend often wore time-
period costumes while at the museum, and Priscilla was curious
which century Mildred would be in today.

Mildred stepped out of the kitchen, her hair piled on top of
her head and her 1850s-style dress emphasizing her thin, tall
frame. She smiled when she spotted Priscilla. "What brings you
here today?"

"Thought I'd see how plans were going for *American Antiques*.
Do you need any help?"

"Other than having everything spic and span for them, there's
not much we're supposed to do." She glanced around the hallway
the themed rooms were built off of. "I'm not sure how many people will actually fit once the show has its camera equipment in
here."

"Guess it's a good thing equipment is getting smaller all the time."

"It'd have to be microscopic to get much of it in here plus people." Mildred frowned as shadows were cast on the floor. "Sun must have gone behind a cloud. I hope they're ready with lots of lighting."

"They will be." The rooms were clean and tidy as usual, everything in its place. "Do you have anything you're going to show the crew?"

"Other than the museum? This is my jewel." Mildred straightened a picture frame where it rested on a doily. "What are you bringing?"

"Nothing from the lighthouse. Gerald helped me look through it yesterday, but I don't have anything to bring."

"It could be great publicity for the lighthouse."

Priscilla nodded. "It could, but if I can't find anything..." She shrugged. When Mildred opened her mouth to argue, Priscilla held up a hand. "I promise I'll think about it. And if you have suggestions, let me know." She hitched her purse strap higher on her shoulder. "And if you end up needing help, just call."

"Thanks. And now I better get back to dusting in the corners."

Mildred was humming as Priscilla left the museum and climbed back in her car. She pulled up the address on her phone and then took her time driving to Wanda's house. Priscilla could see Wanda waiting in the front window as she parked at the end of the drive.

A text beeped on Priscilla's phone. *Come on in. Door's unlocked.*

She didn't even wait for Priscilla to close the front door before she rolled into the hall and asked, "Did you learn anything exciting or important?"

"I did, as a matter of fact. Gerald found out what kind of ship it is."

"Well, don't just stand there." Wanda waved a hand in the air. "Come sit down and tell me all about it."

Priscilla followed Wanda into the living room and sat on the couch. It took only a few minutes to bring the elderly woman up to speed on the latest happenings.

"A lightship? Why didn't I think of that? It's not like I haven't lived on an island for over eighty years. Someday you come visit me, and I'll tell you lots of stories I've heard about lightships."

"That would be wonderful," Priscilla said. "Do you have time to answer a few questions for me?"

"Sure." Wanda slapped the armrest of her wheelchair. "I don't have a lot to do while trapped in this thing."

"Does anyone come to help you?"

Wanda laughed. "I'm not as trapped as all that. I might be eighty-something, but I can get around fine." She moved the chair up and back and around in a circle as if to prove her point. "And the ladies in my church are bringing meals and cleaning for me. So, what do you need to know?"

"Do you have a list or calendar from Renee that tells when people rented your cottage?"

"Somewhere around here." She rolled into the living room and pulled a stack of files from a desk tucked along the wall. It was a beautiful antique secretary that Priscilla hadn't noticed the first time she was there. "This is where I try to keep my accounting papers, but sometimes I wander with them."

She shuffled through the pile a bit. "It has to be here somewhere."

"Can I help you look?"

"Oh no. I can manage it." Wanda spent a few more minutes riffling through the pile before she finally held up a file folder with a triumphant smile. "Here it is."

"Can I compare the lists?"

Wanda looked from the file to Priscilla. "I thought we could peruse them together."

"All right."

"Great." Wanda started rolling back toward the couch.

Priscilla watched her, wondering why Wanda wouldn't simply hand over the list. Why wouldn't she let her compare the lists on her own? Was there something she was concerned Priscilla would see?

CHAPTER TWELVE

Here we go." Two glasses of tea and a small plate of shortbread cookies sat on a tray. Wanda eased the tray to the edge of the coffee table and sank back. "Maybe I'll let you get those. My friend April was here when you called and helped me set this up right before she left."

Priscilla handed Wanda one of the glasses and then took the other. As she did, she noticed that Wanda's folder had ended up beneath the tray when she'd moved it.

"There are a few sugar packets there if you'd like some." Wanda sat back and sighed. "What do you think of my cottage?"

"It's charming. How did it come to be called The Relic?"

"Oh I don't know. Something about the place feeling like it'd been there for a while. I think Renee was the one who actually suggested I name it that. She said the one next to it, Oz, stays full, and part of the draw of a rental is the charming name that makes people think they're getting a piece of something special. It could be a bunch of hooey for all I know, but I like it."

"I do too." Priscilla took a sip of her tea. "I've always admired the campground and its multicolored cottages, but being inside yours was a first, and a treat."

"Each one is unique." Wanda's face took on a faraway look. "I've always thought it would be nice to schedule a tour of the cottages. Donate the money raised to charity. But, I haven't the energy to organize it." She took a sip of her tea. "Well, let's compare these lists."

"I promise we'll keep this short. I just need to confirm that the information Renee gave me matches what she gave you."

"If you're concerned that she's lied to you about this information, why do you think she would give me anything different?"

"I don't know. But it's a place to start." Priscilla picked up a cookie. "I appreciate your help."

"I guess it's the least I can do since I'm the reason you're looking into the ship. I still don't understand how it came to be there."

"I don't either. By the way, did you ask anyone to collect the wooden toys from the cottage for you?"

"What are you talking about?"

"The wooden toys that were stored with the ship are gone."

Wanda frowned, and the wrinkles along her face accentuated. "Do you think this old woman worries about storing toys in a cottage she rents to others?"

"I guess not." Had whoever hidden the toys come back, only to find the model ship missing? "Let's see if we can figure out who might have left them." Priscilla pulled her list onto her lap. "Can I look at yours?"

"Let's read them off. You can tell me what's on your list, and I can confirm if it matches mine."

"Okay." Priscilla drew out the word, then shrugged it off. Maybe it was easier for Wanda this way. "This list shows that the first renter was at the end of May last year. A Darby Jenkins."

"That's right. Memorial Day is when the campground officially opens. We usually don't start until then. The island doesn't get much tourist traffic earlier, so it's not really worth advertising earlier dates."

They proceeded through the list like that. Occasionally Wanda would have a comment to add, but usually it was a quick confirmation. They had almost reached the end when Wanda put her paper down. "I'll put these tea things away."

"I can do that for you." Priscilla moved to take the tray, but Wanda shook her head.

"I also need a powder room break. I'll be right back." She leaned forward and put their tea things on the tray. As she wheeled the tray to the kitchen, Priscilla waited on the couch. Wanda's list sat there right side up, and Priscilla glanced at it. There was an entry on Wanda's list, one for the late fall, after Renee's list ended. And there was a name at the bottom of Renee's list that wasn't on Wanda's.

Priscilla furrowed her brow. Shouldn't Wanda have an accurate list? Didn't she know who was staying in her cabin?

Wanda returned, and Priscilla held up the two lists.

"Why is there a renter on your list that isn't on mine?"

"Oh...um, is there? How funny."

"Wanda, do you want my help?"

"I don't know." She eased the wheelchair closer to Priscilla.

"I can stop if you'd prefer." She certainly had other ways to invest her time other than helping someone who didn't really want help. Especially if Hugh and Marigold pursued their talk of marrying at the lighthouse.

"I'm too old to deal with renting the cottage." Wanda grinned at her, but it looked forced and unnatural. "You might not believe it, but I'm almost eighty-two. I don't want to spend whatever time I have left on this earth messing around with who stays in the cottage and when. But no one else from the family is willing to do it. I need Renee to handle those details, or we can't afford to keep the cottage. It's been in our family for four generations. I'd be heartsick to lose it now."

"But why are you hiding information from her?"

"I don't want to get my son in trouble." Wanda sighed. "But I guess it won't hurt to tell you about it."

"Then let's really compare our lists. Who was this who stayed last at the cottage that's not on Renee's list?"

"Adam Reeling." Wanda glanced at the paper and shrugged. "I don't know him."

"Are you saying that your son set up his stay?"

"Yes. It was after the high season, and my son asked if an acquaintance could use it. I didn't see any harm, especially since he agreed to pay up front. This way we didn't have to give Renee a commission."

"Did you meet Adam? Maybe when he moved in?"

"No. Jerry handled getting him the key." Wanda ran her hand back and forth along the chair's arm. "He handled everything for me. Then sent me the check. That extra income came in handy when we had to replace the water heater and fix the damage around it."

"How long was Adam there?"

"It must have been around September 25 or so—after the Radfords, until the middle of October. Jerry said he had a project he was working on. The man needed a quiet place to work."

"Has anyone stayed there since?"

"Just Jerry and his family over Christmas. I love to have the kids visit, but there's not enough room in this small house to have both of my kids and their families sleep here. One family usually stays at the cabin. Last year it was Jerry's turn."

Priscilla considered this. "Can I have Jerry's information? Maybe he knows about the ship."

Wanda frowned but reached for her phone. She pulled up an entry, and then handed the phone to Priscilla. "Here you go."

"Thanks." Priscilla entered his information in her phone. Then she turned back to the entry she had that Renee hadn't given Wanda. "What do you know about Shellie Leonard?"

"Nothing. Who is she?" Wanda paused and stared off a moment before shaking her head. "I've never heard of her."

Priscilla sighed as she considered what that meant. "I guess I'll pay Renee another visit."

"Can't you just call her?"

"No, it's better to watch her reaction. Often people's bodies say things their words don't."

"Okay. I guess this is why I need your help."

"Do you mind if I look at your list?" Wanda handed it over reluctantly, and Priscilla snapped a picture of it. "Thank you. If you think of anything, feel free to call me, or let Gail know, if that's better."

"Did you know, I met your cousin when she was cleaning these old choppers of mine. We'd talk as she worked, well, I mumbled most of the time. She's become a good friend. You're a lot like her."

"Oh?"

"Yes, the way you're giving of your time for me. Thank you."

Priscilla pushed to her feet. "You're more than welcome," she said. "I'll be in touch."

As she drove back to Vineyard Haven, she thought about all that Wanda had told her and the things she hadn't. While she'd eventually answered questions, there'd been an underlying hesitation that was hard to understand. Why wouldn't she just say that there had been another renter? It was her cabin. She could do what she wanted with it as long as she wasn't breaking the law.

Priscilla almost laughed out loud at the idea. Wanda didn't strike Priscilla as someone who would participate in something nefarious. So why not just come right out with it?

She parked her car and walked back to the association office. The Closed sign was showing, and she frowned. Renee had told her the office hours were until five p.m. or later most nights. Was she trying to take some time off before the season officially kicked off? There really was no reason to think it was anything else, but Priscilla felt the frustration of the loose end as she headed back to her car. She could call Jerry from home, but she wanted to see Renee's reaction to her questions.

A noise at a Pepto Bismol–pink cottage caught her attention, and she turned to find Renee arguing with a painter.

"This is the wrong color. I gave you the color chip."

"And that's what the paint shop color-matched."

"Well, this isn't it." Her frustration was evident from her shrill tone to her fists on her hips.

The man she was talking to wore paint-splattered clothes and a *whatever* expression. "I got what you requested."

Renee clapped her hands on either side of her face and turned away from him. She froze when she spotted Priscilla. "What are you doing back here?"

"I have one more question."

"Of course you do." The words were muttered but reached Priscilla anyway.

"There was an entry on my list of renters that wasn't on Wanda's."

Renee shook her head as if to clear it. "What do you mean?"

"There was an extra entry." Priscilla had decided not to mention Adam Reeling. After all, it was Wanda's cottage. But Renee's mix-up needed to be addressed. "Did Wanda get paid for that week?"

"What? Of course she did," Renee sputtered, brushing past Priscilla. She walked across the street toward the Tabernacle.

Priscilla hurried after her. "She could ask for an audit."

"To what purpose? Spend money neither of us has to prove I didn't keep anything from her?" Renee didn't stop as she crossed through the Tabernacle and to the other side. "That would be a waste of time and money."

"Then explain why there's this discrepancy." Priscilla felt like she was chasing Renee as the woman practically sprinted across the lawn. Good thing Priscilla could be stubborn when it came to getting the answers she needed. "Just be honest with me, and I'll leave."

"Sure you will, until you have another question." Renee stomped up the steps to the porch of the association office. "Look, I will be happy to answer any questions Wanda has. But you aren't the woman I'm working for. I've already wasted time I didn't have to give you what you wanted. If you want more, that's on you."

With that she unlocked the door, went inside, and slammed it in Priscilla's face.

CHAPTER THIRTEEN

Jake was prancing by the door when Priscilla reached her cottage. He looked at her expectantly, trotted to the hook where his leash hung, and gave it a gentle tug. Priscilla laughed and reached down to rub his ears.

"All right, Jake. We'll go for a quick walk down the beach."

She hooked the leash to his collar and grabbed a scarf to add to her barn jacket. This time of year the wind coming off the water could blow right through her in a frigid gust if she wasn't careful. Jake didn't notice the cold, even with his short fur.

As they stepped down the wooden stairs leading from the lighthouse to the narrow beach, Priscilla imagined how she should approach Jerry. Wanda's son would likely be skeptical about why she was calling, but she hadn't wanted Wanda to alert him ahead of time. She wouldn't be able to see his reaction, but she could try to get an unvarnished response to her questions.

That shouldn't be so hard, but it seemed the people she was approaching all had something they didn't want to be forthcoming about.

After letting Jake stretch his legs and dig for clams, Priscilla climbed the stairs to the cottage. Once inside, she got her dog a fresh bowl of water and laughed as he went to town slurping it up.

She'd have to mop up the floor around his bowl, but when he plopped down with a happy doggie smile, she couldn't help grinning back at him.

She grabbed a glass of tea for herself, as well as her notes and a pencil, and then sat at the small kitchen table. She sipped the tea, then pulled out her phone and tapped on Jerry's phone number.

The phone rang for a minute before a man answered. "Hello?"

"Is this Jerry Shire?"

"It is." His voice was cautious, and Priscilla hurried on before he could hang up.

"My name is Priscilla Grant, and I'm helping your mom with something we found in the Relic."

"Okay..."

"*American Antiques* is coming to the island this weekend, and your mom asked my cousin and me to look through her cottage for items that might be of interest to the hosts."

He groaned good-naturedly. "My mom loves that show. Thinks Tim and Cherish are amazing."

"Well, when we were looking through the cottage, I found a large three-foot-long metal ship. Your mom doesn't recognize it."

"A metal ship? Where did you find it?"

"In the twin bedroom. Wrapped up in a blanket and tucked in a dresser drawer."

"Huh."

She let his word settle, hoping he would continue, but he was silent. "I wondered if you might recognize it."

"I can't imagine I would. The last time I stayed there was in December, and most of our time was spent at Mom's. The cottage is on the small side, and my family and I minimized our time there." He sighed. "It's not winterized, so it gets cold."

"I'm sure it does." The winter winds could cut right across the island, and even with the proper insulation, it could feel bitter on the right night. "Do you mind if I send you a photo of it?"

"I can show it to my boys, who stayed in that room."

"Great." She changed tack. "Your mom also told me you arranged the final renter of the year."

"She did?"

"Yes." Priscilla glanced at her notes. "I think his name was Adam Reeling."

"Huh." There was a pause as if he was considering the name. "I know who you mean. He's an acquaintance of mine."

"How long did he stay at the cottage?"

"I'm not sure how that's relevant to anything, but he was there three or four weeks starting in the shoulder season."

Priscilla tapped her pencil against the table. "Do you know what he needed the cottage for?"

"He said he needed a fresh place to focus on a project. He's single, so there was plenty of room, and his needs were pretty minimal."

"Okay." Priscilla doodled on the edge of her notes. "Do you know why he wanted the cottage for such a long period?"

"Beyond what I just said, no."

"All right. I'll text you the photo. Would you mind checking with him too?"

"I don't think that's necessary."

She sighed. "I've been calling last year's renters. If you give me his information, I can contact him, and you won't have to do anything."

"Is it really important?"

"Honestly? I don't know. I know that there is a large model ship that was left in your mom's cottage, and she doesn't recognize it. We don't know who it belongs to, and that makes it hard to return it to where it belongs."

"Maybe it's not supposed to be returned."

"Why leave it there in the first place?"

There were voices in the background. "Look, I've gotta go. Send me the photo, and I'll look at it."

"Thanks."

He hung up, and Priscilla realized he'd avoided her request for Adam's information. She quickly composed a text to him with the photo and asked again. She sank back against the chair and took a long drink of her tea.

Jake licked her hand, and she ruffled his fur and pushed him away with a smile. "Silly boy. I guess I'll work on chores and pray for inspiration."

The next hour passed as she cleaned, and her mind wandered over what she had learned. The ship was not willingly giving up its secrets, and the people she'd talked to seemed reluctant to do the same. No one else had returned her calls and emails. And, after what she'd learned from Gerald, a secret part of her hoped no one would claim it. What a great addition to her lighthouse museum it would be!

She'd shown the photo to enough people, she was surprised no one had recognized it.

Maybe someone at an antique store would know its value. Would this be something that Willow Gibson, the owner of Silver Willow Appraisals and Antiques, could help her with? She'd met Willow almost two years ago, and if she remembered correctly, her antiques shop dealt primarily in estates, but maybe she'd run across valuable toys or models in that context. It would be worth a call or a visit to her shop.

Priscilla glanced at her watch and saw that it was after five. It might not hurt to call Willow, but her shop was probably closed at this hour. It only took a minute to look up the Silver Willow phone number. When she dialed, it rang through to voice mail. Priscilla left a message and then turned to her laptop. Maybe one of the renters had returned her email. So far she'd only had replies from Luke Brainerd and Nathan Radford.

New emails downloaded, and she found one from a Margie Throne. It was a quick note.

Hello, Priscilla. My family and I stayed in the cabin the week of July 4th. My children had some toys, but nothing was left behind that we know of. If there's anything further you need, feel free to call me at this number.

Priscilla dialed the number, and a moment later a woman answered.

"Is this Margie Throne?" After the woman confirmed that she was, indeed, Margie Throne, Priscilla continued. "Thanks so much for emailing me back about your stay at the Relic on Martha's Vineyard."

"My kids still talk about that tiny space. You'd think living in a Boston brownstone apartment, they'd be used to small, but guess not."

Brownstone would translate to pricey. Would the family even worry about having lost the ship? "Did your kids travel with many toys?"

"Not really. We wanted to unplug and focus on the island. We all needed a break from the city. Why do you ask?"

"As I mentioned in my email, we found a ship in the cottage that might have been left by a renter. If so, we're trying to figure out who so we can return it."

"Wow. That's considerate of you. Not many people would go to the trouble for strangers."

Priscilla sighed. "It's a bit oversized, so it would be good to find its home. It might be a family heirloom. It would be helpful to know if it's valuable or not. Then we'd know if we should keep looking for the owner."

"I have an idea that might help. I have friends who go antiquing all the time. When they find something they need appraised, they call either Shondra Johnson or Bob Gothard, both of them here in Boston. I'm pretty sure one of them could help you."

"Thank you. I'll give them a call."

"Excuse me a moment." The woman answered someone's question, then came back. "I'm sorry I can't be more help."

"Actually, confirming you were in the cottage that week helps." At least she knew that entry was correct on Renee's list. "Thank you for your time."

After she hung up, Priscilla tried to consider whether it was worth continuing her pursuit of the ship's owner. If a guest had left the ship and valued it, they would have already called and arranged to collect it.

At least she could confirm the dates that three of the prior year's renters had been at the cabin. The calendar still had large gaps, but it was slowly filling in. If she could uncover the ship's origins and get the pieces to fill in there, maybe the rest would make sense.

And tomorrow morning she'd start with Willow. If Willow couldn't help her, she'd try Bob Gothard. And if Bob Gothard couldn't help her, she'd try Shondra Johnson. And if Shondra Johnson couldn't help her, she'd forget the whole thing and tell Wanda to find an old cake stand or something to present to Tim and Cherish. By the time Gerald called, she'd almost convinced herself that was exactly what she'd do.

CHAPTER FOURTEEN

The air smelled of sea salt as Priscilla walked along Manexit Road in Vineyard Haven. The Silver Willow had an address on that street, but couldn't be seen directly from the road.

The Silver Willow's white siding was a nice complement to the darker roof, though the plate glass window next to the door was in desperate need of a good cleaning. Willow, a slightly heavyset woman with expertly styled, shoulder-length blonde hair, was turning the sign to Open when Priscilla walked up.

Willow paused midturn and considered Priscilla before a smile of recognition dawned on her face. She released the sign and opened the door.

"My, I didn't expect to see you today. It's Priscilla Grant, right?"

"Yes." Priscilla extended her hand to shake Willow's. "It's good to see you again. Do you have a moment, or am I too early to ask your opinion on something?"

Willow shook her head and made a sweeping gesture with a well-manicured hand. "Please, come on in. I don't have an appointment for forty-five minutes. How can I help you today?"

Priscilla had to smile. Willow was much more eager to help her than she had been the first time they'd met when Priscilla had brought questions to her about a medal given to a WASP for her service during World War II. It would be nice if she stayed helpful and interested. "I've been helping a new friend who has a cottage on the Martha's Vineyard Camp Meeting Association grounds. We were looking for something for her, and I found this instead." Priscilla pulled up the photo of the ship on her phone and held it out to Willow. "Can you help me learn more about it?"

Willow pulled reading glasses from the top of her head and studied the photo, manipulating the size. "What do you need to know?"

"The cottage's owner doesn't recognize the ship."

"Okay...?"

"I'm trying to reach the various renters from last summer, but having more information about it might help me find the owner more quickly."

"Assuming they care and want to be found. I can't tell you how many times someone comes to me with an estate item that they swear is valuable, and I have to explain the realities of the market. Sometimes they're right, and they've got an amazing find on their hands. Most of the time its value is found in the family lore." She handed Priscilla back her phone and led the way to a beautiful antique couch. "Let's see what we can do though. How big is the ship?"

"Roughly three feet long and about sixteen inches tall with the masts."

"That's a large ship. Metal?"

"Yes. It's a Coast Guard lightship. Isn't that interesting? I didn't even know such a thing existed."

"I've never heard of those either. Can you email me the photos?" Willow handed Priscilla her business card.

"Sure. Any thoughts on what to do next?"

"I'll try to see what I can find, but I also have a few contacts who deal largely in toys and models. Is it okay if I consult them?"

"Yes, that would be fine. I was going to ask if you've heard of a Shonda Johnson or Bob Gothard in Boston."

"I have. I can add them to my list to call, if you'd like. Would it be all right with you if I forwarded the photos to them?"

"Or I can do that."

"Let me check first. I don't want to waste your time, and it'll give me a good excuse to reconnect with them, stay in the front of their minds." She stood and moved to her desk and jotted a note on her desk calendar. "Give me a couple of hours, and I should have some good information or someone who's willing to look at it." Willow tapped her pen against the notepad. "Who did you say the owner of the cottage is?"

"I didn't. She'd like to remain anonymous until we determine whether it's hers to keep."

"Sounds like a story." Willow glanced at her watch, an antique that dangled from a chain around her neck. "I need to get ready for my meeting. I've got a fresh estate coming in. Sounds like they have some interesting items to move along. I'll make those calls after I'm done with that."

"Thanks for your time, and I'll look forward to your call." Priscilla made sure Willow had her phone number, and then wandered through the small shop on her way back out.

Willow had added a small display area on one side for representative antiques. The pieces were displayed in a way that the individual items made a cohesive image. A craftsman sideboard was next to a Louis XV chair on top of a Persian rug. An artful pile of old leather books sat on the edge of the sideboard, and a painting that looked like an Audubon hung over it. It looked like the business had grown since the last time she'd consulted with Willow.

"Are you looking for anything for your cottage while you're here?" Willow's question pulled Priscilla from her perusal of the books.

"No. I enjoy looking at what you've acquired though. The shop seems changed from the last time I was here."

"It should, since I've turned the inventory several times. I enjoy the hunt and matching the right item with the right person." Willow ran a finger over a piece of furniture and then inspected her finger for dust. "If you decide you want something, keep me in mind."

"I will. Thanks again."

Once outside Priscilla lifted her face to the sun. Then she walked up the alley back toward her car, but decided to make a detour to Candy's. The pastry shop was only a few blocks away and one of her favorite places to stop. The only question was what to get when she arrived. The cranberry muffins were a personal favorite, but on a late spring day, a cruller dunked in coffee sounded good too.

A few minutes later Priscilla walked into the bakery and was greeted by the subtle aroma of Candy's famous love cookies—

rosemary shortbread cookies dusted in powdered sugar—along with the delectable smell of flavored coffee.

Candy popped up from behind the counter with a smile on her face that hadn't altered since she'd eloped with Beau Ortmann a couple of months earlier. Her eyes sparkled as she wiped her hands on her apron. "What can I get for you today, Priscilla?"

"Are you experimenting with anything seasonal?" Sometimes Candy had samples of new recipes she was fine-tuning.

"I'm sticking with the standards right now. Guess I'm distracted." She giggled as her rings flashed on her hand.

"That's understandable." Priscilla glanced over the contents of the bakery case. "How about a cruller and hazelnut coffee?"

Candy leaned down and pulled out a cruller. "Here or to go?"

Priscilla glanced at the small section with café seating. With only half the tables filled, there was plenty of room to settle in and enjoy the treat. "I'll stay."

"Perfect." Candy set the cruller on a plate, then placed that on top of the case before turning to fill a mug from one of the carafes lined up behind the counter. "Here you go."

Priscilla made her way to an empty table and sat down as Candy grabbed a damp towel and began wiping down tables. "Have you heard about *American Antiques* coming to the island Saturday?"

Candy nodded. "They've asked me to cater a continental breakfast."

"What a great idea."

"I don't mind doing it, but it seems like the catering side of my business could explode. That will be hard to maintain without more year-round help."

"That sounds like a good problem to me." Priscilla smiled at the lopsided grimace Candy made. "Have you heard chatter about the show? Are people searching their homes for items?"

"I'm not. Are you?"

"Well, I didn't find anything at my house, but Gail and I found something interesting in Wanda Shire's cabin on the campgrounds that might be worth showing Tim and Cherish."

"Those cabins are so cute. Did I tell you that Beau and I actually rented one of the cabins for our belated honeymoon a couple of weeks ago?"

"You did? Which one did you stay in?"

"We originally wanted to stay in the Sunny Bunch—we'd heard that one was newly renovated and perfect for honeymooning, but the lady there told us it was already booked, so we took the one called Martha's Mate."

Priscilla dunked her cruller in her coffee and took a bite. Heaven. "How did you enjoy it?"

"It was wonderful and blissful, just like a honeymoon should be." Candy frowned. "But you know, it was the funniest thing. Martha's Mate was just a couple of cabins away from the Sunny Bunch, and we didn't see anyone there the whole weekend. No car, no people, no activity at all, never a light on. We couldn't understand it."

The front door opened, and Candy straightened. "I'm the only one here right now, so I'd better get that."

"Of course. Thanks for the treats."

"My pleasure." Candy winked and then sashayed to the counter where her new husband waited with a grin on his face. "What can I get you today?"

He pulled her to his side and kissed her. "I've already got what I want."

Candy blushed and giggled as she moved behind the counter and got a coffee for him.

Priscilla watched them with a smile on her face. It was good to see them together, enjoying the blush of young married love. She and Gary had experienced days where just the sight of each other was enough to keep them warm and happy. She took the last bite of the cruller and washed it down with the coffee. She missed Gary, but she didn't ache like she used to. She had built a life on the island that allowed her to honor the past while wondering what the future could bring.

She collected her plate and cup and put them in the tub on the trashcan. Then she waved at Candy as she headed outside. The walk to her car was pleasant with the sun still out and warming her face.

As she settled into her car, her phone buzzed with a text.

Willow had some news.

CHAPTER FIFTEEN

The text was short and to the point.

Both Bob Gothard and Shondra Johnson deal with toys and have an expertise that could be helpful. They're expecting your call. Hope they can help. Willow listed the contact information for both dealers below her breezy text.

Priscilla set her phone aside and backed her car onto the road. The drive from Candy's back to her cottage was quick as she organized her thoughts about what she wanted to learn from the antiques appraisers. While she might learn the value of the ship on Saturday, she wondered if knowing that information now would give her any insight that would help her track down who had left it at Wanda's cottage. It would surely let her know whether to encourage Wanda to take it to the show or leave it behind.

As she drove, she puzzled over what Candy had told her about the empty cabin. Why would Renee tell them the Sunny Bunch was booked when it wasn't? So now not only was she booking people into cabins without informing the owners, she was telling potential customers that cabins were booked when they weren't. In the first instance, she could collect the entire rental fee for herself, and Priscilla could see the temptation in that. But lying about a cottage's availability? What did Renee have to gain by that?

When Priscilla reached home, she let Jake out and then pulled out her laptop. It only took a minute to look up the two antiques experts. On the drive home, she'd decided she wasn't going to tell them that she knew the model was a lightship. If they found that out on their own, that was a way to prove their expertise to her.

Shondra Johnson's photo on her website showed a woman who appeared to be in her late forties. She had brown hair that curled around her long face, and green eyes that sparked with intelligence. She wore a pastel sweater and smiled as she looked straight into the camera. Her bio listed classes and training she'd received that qualified her to appraise estates. When Priscilla clicked around her website, she located a few pages about antique model airplanes and cars. Hopefully her expertise would translate to model ships.

Then she pulled up information on the second expert. Bob Gothard looked to be in his midsixties. His shop was called the Toy Menagerie, and he seemed to declare himself an expert. His bio was spare on details, but he had pages of photos and information about toys. One page was dedicated to toy ships. While none of them looked like the one she'd found, and she wasn't all that convinced that the ship was a toy, he seemed like the right person to start with.

While she'd love to take the ship to him, he was more than two hours away on the mainland near Boston. When she dialed the number listed on the website, a young woman answered.

"The Toy Menagerie. How can I help you?"

"Hello, I'm calling for Bob Gothard."

"Just a moment." The woman might have pulled the phone from her ear, but Priscilla still cringed when she yelled. "Bob, phone's for you." There was a muffled reply, and then she was back on the phone. "He'll be right with you."

"Thanks."

A minute later a man got on the phone. "This is Bob."

"Hi, Bob. I'm Priscilla Grant, and we share a mutual friend, Willow Gibson."

"Sure, she told me you might call."

"Do you have a minute?" After he said he did, she gave him the background on the ship. "I can't find anything that helps me identify it, but Willow thought you might be able to help since you're an expert on toys."

"I don't know that anyone can truly be an expert, but I do spend my time playing with them."

"Have you had any training in appraising toys?"

"Sure have." He launched into a list of letters and acronyms that meant nothing to her.

When he paused for breath she jumped back in. "How should we proceed?"

"Willow sent me some photos. Won't take me long to tell if it's worth anything."

She hung up and turned to the next call. Maybe Shondra Johnson would be similarly helpful.

This time the phone rang and rang, and just before she was going to hang up, a woman answered. "Hello? Are you still there?"

"I am."

"Oh good, I hate to make people wait while the phone rings, but I was elbow deep in wood wax. I needed to strip off my gloves before I picked up the phone. Anyway, you didn't call to hear that." She chuckled self-consciously. "How can I help you?"

"My name is Priscilla Grant. Willow Gibson is an acquaintance of mine on Martha's Vineyard, and she suggested I call you."

"Ah. She mentioned someone who had found something interesting. I guess that was you."

"When I was helping a friend of mine look through her cabin, I found a large metal ship. She's not familiar with it, so we're trying to learn more so we can decide what to do with it."

"Is it a model or a toy?"

"We really aren't sure, but it seems more like a large model than a toy."

"I have the pictures Willow sent me. Tell me more about it, and then I'll know whether I can help."

Priscilla described the general proportions and the details of the ship.

Shondra repeated some of the details, obviously taking notes. "Any sort of manufacturer's markings?"

"I didn't find any."

"No words?"

"Not that I can make out."

"Okay. You've got me curious. I don't deal specifically with ships, but I might have some ideas."

"Thank you."

"Sure. Willow's helped me on occasion, so I'm glad to do the same for you."

After Priscilla hung up, she checked her email again. Still no reply from the other renters she'd emailed. Was it possible they weren't real renters? It seemed a little crazy, but to have so many not return her emails made her wonder. She sent several of them a second email to check. Then she sank back and considered her next steps.

Maybe she needed to focus on something else for a bit. The question was...what?

It had been a while since she'd talked to Rachel. This would be a good opportunity to connect with her and see how she was settling into Boston. Priscilla smiled at the thought that her only child was just a couple of hours away after the year they'd been separated by the many miles between Kansas and Martha's Vineyard.

Rachel picked up quickly. "Hey, Mom."

"Hi, Rachel. Thought I'd call and see how things are going. Need any help with the wedding plans?"

"You've helped so much already, and we appreciate it. We've got everything else under control."

"Are you sure?"

"I'm sure. In a couple of weeks when we start getting RSVPs— that's when I'll need you desperately." She laughed.

"I feel like I should be more harried. As the mother of the bride, I thought that was my role."

Rachel laughed again. "I'm good, Mom. Don't worry. I'll ask for help when I need it, but right now it's hurry-up-and-wait time.

Enjoy the down time while you can." She sighed. "Maybe you'd like to come finish unpacking for me?"

Now Priscilla laughed. "You had almost all your boxes unpacked before the moving van left."

"But I haven't done a thing since. I just can't get motivated. What with the new job and new city, unpacking is the last thing on my priority list."

Priscilla shifted on the couch to get more comfortable. "Not to mention a fiancé. How are you liking Boston?"

"I really like it here, Mom. It's so different, but it's good."

"I agree. How's the job going?"

Rachel launched into a description of a sales pitch meeting she'd attended with her colleagues. "You should have seen everyone's jaw drop when the slide came up with the wrong client logo on it. I don't think we'll get that contract. I'm just glad I was observing and not part of the presentation. I felt so bad for them." She paused. "I hope they'll ask for more help proofing after this though."

"Ouch. Sounds like they need you. You're the detail queen."

"Yeah. It was bad, and I'd like to help them avoid a repeat performance. Hey, would it be okay if I came to the island this weekend? I'm not sure it will work yet, but I'd like to try."

"You're always welcome. There's a bit of excitement this weekend." Priscilla stood and walked to the kitchen where she turned on the burner under the teakettle. "*American Antiques* will be here to shoot an episode."

"Really? That sounds like fun."

"It could be. I was helping Gail search a friend's cabin for something to take to the taping."

"Oh?"

"I found a large model ship, but I'm not sure it's really worth anything. I can't find out anything about it."

"Why's that? Doesn't Gail's friend know where it came from?"

"No." Priscilla knew it sounded slightly crazy, especially when Rachel put it like that. "I thought we'd ask the cottage's owner about it, and boom! Mystery solved."

"You'll get there, Mom. I'll let you know by Thursday night if I'm able to come."

"Sounds good. You know I'd love to have you." The teakettle started whistling, and Priscilla stood and hurried to the kitchen to pull a mug from the cupboard. She selected a teabag and poured the hot water over it. "Love you." She pulled a box of brownie mix from the cabinet along with the other ingredients. Something chocolate sounded good, though she wished she had someone to share the 9 × 9 pan of sweetness with.

"Love you too. I promise I'll be in touch."

After the call ended, Priscilla mixed the brownies and tucked the pan in the oven before carrying her mug to the little bistro table and settling down with a book. Jake plopped at her feet and whined, but she looked at him and shook her head. "Not now, boy. I'm going to read while the brownies are in the oven."

The mystery novel held her attention for a while, and then her gaze wandered to the other room as her thoughts returned to the ship.

She knew from experience it only took one clue or comment to unlock hidden details. What had the ship been used for? It wasn't dotted with rust, so she doubted it had spent much time in water. Even if someone had tried, it was solid enough to sink. So was it primarily decorative?

It probably didn't matter. Wanda wanted to know who to return it to, and Priscilla was curious about whether it had hidden value.

What if it had been hidden in the cottage with no intention of it being found?

The thought made her frown, because if it had been hidden there, the person had to know it would eventually be found. Unless they planned to come back to claim it before the season started. The thought thrummed through her mind.

Could it be something as simple as that? But if so, why hide it in Wanda's cabin?

CHAPTER SIXTEEN

The sun was setting when Priscilla began preparing a light supper. Her phone rang, and Gail was on the other end. "Priscilla, is there any chance you can come over for dinner?"

"It depends on what you're having." Gail sputtered, and Priscilla laughed. "Just kidding. I was just making soup and salad here, so I'm sure whatever you have will be better."

"No pressure." Gail sighed. "Marigold will be here too."

"And Tommy?"

"Of course."

"I'll be there shortly."

It wasn't a long drive down Old Lighthouse Road and onto Fairfield to reach the house Gail shared with her dad. When Priscilla arrived Tommy Townsend's truck was in the driveway, so she pulled alongside the curb. Priscilla grabbed the plate of brownies she'd brought along and hurried up the walk to the small house. When she knocked, someone called for her to come on in.

Tommy greeted her. "Hi, Priscilla. Glad you're here."

"Thanks, Tommy." She slipped her shoes off and followed him to the kitchen. Marigold and Hugh sat at the table, while Gail pulled a pan of lasagna out of the oven.

Gail turned toward Priscilla, and her smile broadened when she spotted the brownies. "I didn't have anything for dessert yet."

"They aren't anything fancy, but I made them earlier this afternoon. I didn't want to eat them all." She placed them on the counter next to the stove. "How can I help?"

"Tell Marigold here that we don't need a big wedding." Uncle Hugh's voice held a note of teasing, but tension seemed to hang between the couple.

"I only want close friends and our families." Marigold's lower lip pouted out.

Uncle Hugh held up his hand to shield one side of his mouth and winked. "I think my girl believes half the island fits that description."

"There's lots of room on the lighthouse grounds." Priscilla held up her hands in a placating motion.

"For two hundred?" Hugh reached across the table and took Marigold's hand.

"I think so. Parking will be the only issue, but you can ask people to carpool."

Marigold shook her head with a wry smile. "I don't think we'll have that many people. We're talking about having this in five days, Hugh."

"As long as we're committing to each other for the rest of our days, I don't care who's there."

Gail watched her father with misty eyes, while Tommy watched her. Priscilla hoped that something more concrete would happen between her cousin and Tommy now that their parents would be together, but they needed to take things in order.

She pulled her gaze back to Marigold. "Just let me know what you need."

"Right now, I need everyone to eat." Gail cut the lasagna into squares that she dished onto plates. She added a slice of buttered French bread to each while Tommy tossed green beans in some olive oil and salt. The air was filled with the aroma of garlic, tomato, and Italian seasonings. Priscilla's stomach growled in response.

They sat at the table and said a simple grace, and as they started eating, Priscilla asked a few questions about colors and flowers, but Marigold didn't have strong opinions. Instead, she was focused on the people she wanted in attendance. Priscilla loved that. It seemed appropriate for a later-in-life wedding that the bride would care more about people than appearances. After all, it was the result that mattered more than the details of the proceedings.

The conversation around the table was freewheeling, and Priscilla enjoyed sharing the meal with them. Over mugs of decaf coffee and the brownies, Priscilla turned to Marigold. "Do you know Wanda Shire? She has a cottage over at the Martha's Vineyard Camp Meeting Association."

Marigold looked at Uncle Hugh, who shrugged. "Wanda lives over near Edgartown, right?"

"Yes."

Gail leaned forward on the table. "I've known her for years. She's a patient at the dental office. Dad, how did you first meet her?"

"Can't think of a beginning time. Seems like I've always known her. She was good friends with your mom, Gail."

"That's right." Gail turned to Marigold. "Do you know her?"

Marigold nodded. "Is her cottage named 'The Relic'?"

"It is," Priscilla confirmed.

"Then yes, I know her." Marigold shifted in her seat as if trying to find a comfortable spot. "Is that who you were helping over the weekend, Gail?"

Gail nodded. "She had surgery a little over a week ago and has only been home a few days."

Marigold glanced at her son. "Hmm. Tommy, remember when she asked us for someone to do some repairs at her cottage over the winter?"

Tommy nodded. "I recommended Beau Ortmann. He does good work when you need a handyman."

"I wonder if she had him come in. Sounded like she had quite the list of odds-and-ends repairs."

Tommy nodded. "She needed everything ready for this year's season. Keeping those cottages isn't cheap. Many of them are a hundred years old, and the upkeep gets steep. If you aren't independently wealthy, it can be a challenge to afford them. Even losing a couple weeks of the season can be the difference between being able to keep your cottage and having to sell it."

"I'm sure that cottage has been paid off for years." Marigold leaned back from the table. "Remember when my family had a cottage there? It was tucked in a corner and such a nice place."

"What happened to it?" Priscilla asked.

"My siblings and I decided to sell it when our parents died. It was too much after we'd scattered around the country, and I couldn't afford it on my own. That's where Wanda finds herself now, I'd imagine."

"Did you have maintenance issues with yours?"

"Of course." Marigold pleated her napkin. "Those cottages are historic, and that means roofs have to be replaced, paint has to be updated, and the insides need to be improved to meet today's expectations while maintaining ties to the past. The rules when it comes to maintaining a historic landmark are overwhelming."

Uncle Hugh guffawed and nudged Marigold's shoulder. "Kind of like us."

She frowned at him, but then softened it to a smile. "I like to think of myself as well preserved."

"You are, my dear."

A soft blush colored her cheeks, and Priscilla exchanged a glance with Gail. She turned back to Marigold. "What's Wanda like? I've barely gotten to know her, but she seems like a nice woman."

"Oh, she is. Just scatterbrained, and that's getting worse as she gets older. She's the type of person you have to call the day of to remind about a meeting that was scheduled ahead of time. But when you're with her, she's a delight."

"Do you think she'd forget about something she put her in cottage?"

"Like the item you found?"

"Yes."

Marigold met Uncle Hugh's gaze, and he shrugged. "I don't know," Marigold said. "It's not like she has dementia. She's just not bothered with details."

"Lives in the moment," Uncle Hugh inserted with a nod.

"Exactly. She's got a laser focus on the things that interest her. I'm not sure the cottage or its contents would qualify."

Priscilla considered that, then thought about Renee. "Did you and your family ever work with Renee Overman?" she asked Marigold.

"Who?"

"She runs the association office at the campground."

"Nope. She must have started after we left. Why?"

"I'm not sure about her, but need a second opinion." Priscilla knew the value of comparing her take on a person or situation with that of someone else.

Marigold shook her head. "Sorry I can't help."

Tommy jumped in with an anecdote about something that happened at his job, and the rest of the evening passed enjoyably as they played a rousing game of Clue.

Priscilla gave Gail a hug before she headed to the door. "Thanks for inviting me."

"I'm glad spontaneous worked." Gail glanced back at her dad and Marigold. "They needed someone to distract them at the beginning. I wasn't cutting it."

"The wedding will be behind you on Sunday evening."

"If they don't kill me with their bickering in the meantime." She shook off the melancholy and opened the door. "Friday, Joan and Trudy are joining me at the Coast Guard station in the morning."

"Oh?"

"The Chilmark students will have their Memorial Day event there this year. Then we thought we'd watch other students in the March to the Sea Parade."

"I missed those last year."

"Then join us. Those are some of the simple events that make living on the island special. There will be some tourists, but mostly they're local events."

"Sounds good."

"We'll pick you up on the way to Menemsha."

Priscilla had a lot to think about on the drive home. She might not have learned anything more about Renee, but that could be misplaced concern on her part.

She would need to spend time on the yard tomorrow to get it ready for Hugh and Marigold's day. The riding mower helped as she mowed the acres around the lighthouse, cottage, and drive. But she also wanted to finish the flowerbeds and maybe get some potted plants that would provide bright splashes of color.

Maybe marigolds would work—if she could arrange them with some taller plants and keep it from looking like a joke related to Marigold's name. It might be too early in the season for those, but Priscilla knew she could find something perfect to incorporate into her landscaping around the lighthouse after the ceremony. So far, she'd only put time and attention into the beds around her cottage.

She knew the Vineyard Garden Nursery would have something she could use among its selection of annuals and perennials. She could spend time enjoying the variety while she decided what would be best. She went to bed satisfied with her plan—after making Gerald listen to her ideas and submit a few of his own.

Wednesday morning Priscilla put Jake into her SUV and headed toward West Tisbury and the garden center. Jake would enjoy the time sniffing around the plants, and she wouldn't feel so guilty about leaving him again. She rolled the passenger window down about halfway, and Jake stuck his head out the window with a happy doggie grin, his tongue hanging out and flapping in the wind.

When she parked, Jake moved to her side and then back to the window in an excited dance.

"Calm down, boy. Don't make me regret bringing you."

Jake seemed to understand her words, because he sat still while she got out and walked around to let him out. Once she had a firm grip on his leash, she grabbed her purse and headed toward the outdoor rows of plants. They strolled past the hydrangeas followed by a variety of colorful roses. Then there were hostas with broad leaves, heuchera with its colored, heavily veined leaves and red bell-like flowers, astilbe with its tall pink and red spikes of flowers, and salvia in butterfly-attracting colors.

There wasn't much shade around the lighthouse, so the hostas wouldn't be a great choice, but the idea of some medium-sized hydrangeas that could grow over future summers mixed with some smaller heuchera and astilbes could be beautiful. She could also get a few roses to put in pretty pots for the wedding and then plant by the stairs to the beach later.

An image was beginning to form in her mind, and she loved it. Then Jake tugged her toward another row with smaller annuals. "Jake, quit pulling."

But Jake didn't listen, and as he tugged her around the corner, she spotted Renee standing next to a tall older man, whose menacing stance seemed to overwhelm her.

CHAPTER SEVENTEEN

The man stepped closer, and Renee had nowhere to go as her back hit a table topped with small six-packs of flowers. Renee seemed to shrink deeper into herself as he edged closer.

Jake growled low in his throat, and the man jerked toward them.

Priscilla pasted a smile on her face and started walking that direction. "Hi, Renee." Renee's face flared with panic, but Priscilla kept approaching. "I don't think I've met your friend."

"You haven't." Renee made a small movement with her hand as if urging Priscilla to back away.

The man turned his attention to Priscilla. "You are?"

"A friend."

He grunted, then said in his thick Boston accent, "You have two days, Overman."

Then he turned and left, his steps clipped as he strode his way down the aisle.

Renee didn't relax until he turned the corner and disappeared. "Why did you do that?"

"I don't like bullies."

"He's not a nice man."

"Then what were you doing with him?"

"Trust me, if I could avoid him, I would." Renee rubbed her arms as she looked away from Priscilla. "You really shouldn't have interfered."

"What was he trying to do?"

"He wants something." She shrugged. "Anyway, what are you doing here?"

"Looking for some plants." Priscilla gestured toward her long cart loaded with the plants she'd selected. "What does he want from you?"

"Something he left. And no, it's not what you found." While the words were forceful, Renee's tone was anything but. She didn't sound certain at all.

"Where did he leave this thing?"

"In a cottage. He's forgetting that working there doesn't mean I have access to all of the cottages. Most of the owners don't leave keys with the association. They're privately owned and maintained unless there's a problem." Renee closed her eyes and gave herself a shake, and when she opened her eyes again, she seemed to have recovered her equilibrium.

Her words didn't ring true to Priscilla. "If you're in trouble, I can help."

Renee snorted as she turned away. "You can't fix everything, Priscilla. Some things are just out of your control."

"Was he a guest at one of the cottages?"

"He might call it that, but most people wouldn't."

"What do you mean?"

"Let's just say, he didn't pay rent."

Priscilla glanced toward the direction where the man had disappeared. Hopefully, he'd kept going. But when she exited fifteen minutes later with her large cart filled with plants, she noticed him sitting in a black Audi tucked under a tree. He was staring at the front door of the garden center as if waiting for Renee to come out, but then his attention flicked to Priscilla, and she felt its force.

Just then, one of the garden center's employees hurried toward her. "Ms. Grant, you forgot your credit card." The young man stopped in front of her and handed her the card.

"My goodness, I don't know when I would have noticed." She relaxed a bit with his presence. "Thank you."

"Can I help you load the plants in your car?"

"That would be a great help."

As she watched the friendly employee load the plants, she kept the man in the periphery of her gaze. She felt a little better having the young employee with her. At least she wasn't alone wondering if the man would jump from his car and want to continue their conversation. As she thanked the teenager for his help, she pivoted and tried to memorize the license plate number on the front of the car. Then she hurriedly sat in her car and repeated the number to herself as she looked for a piece of paper.

The man got out of his car and started moving toward her, so she locked the car doors and jotted the license number on a napkin. He stopped coming toward her when she started the car and pulled out.

During the drive back to town, Priscilla kept an eye on the rearview mirror but didn't see the black Audi. Her thoughts roamed over what Renee had told her, looking for what the office manager hadn't said. It sounded like the man had used at least one of the cottages without permission.

Could he have been in Wanda's cabin? If so, why? How could he have used it without paying rent? Wouldn't Renee have stopped him?

In the off-season, Renee would know which cabins were unlikely to be used. She would know where someone could stay in a cottage unnoticed. Or which ones they could hide items in. It would certainly explain why some cabins, like the Sunny Bunch, would be "booked" but not occupied.

What would they hide, and why?

Was there a ring of thieves stealing or hiding items on the island? The idea felt farfetched. Would something like the ship be part of that? It just didn't strike Priscilla as something worth stealing and then transporting to an out-of-the-way island, although it would very likely stay hidden if it was moved to Martha's Vineyard.

Maybe she was onto something. Instead of going home, she turned to go to the Tisbury Police Station. Maybe Chief Hank Westin would be in, and she could run what felt like a crazy idea past him. He'd let her know if she was overthinking everything.

She was relieved to pull into a shaded spot in the parking lot tucked next to the white clapboard building. She cracked the windows a couple of inches, then turned to Jake. "Stay here, boy. I'll be back in a minute."

He turned a circle on the seat and then settled in, the breeze entering the car teasing his fur.

A minute later she hurried up the stairs to the main door, the napkin with the license plate number clutched in her hand. Gabrielle Grimes sat at the front desk when Priscilla walked inside.

The receptionist pushed her thick-framed glasses up her nose as she turned from her computer to Priscilla. "Priscilla, how can I help you today?" Then she squinted at Priscilla. "You look white as a ghost. Everything okay?"

"I think so. Is Chief Westin in?"

"He's in some bigwig meeting with the mayor. I can assure you, he'd rather be here to meet with you."

"How about Officer April Brown?"

"I think she's back from patrol." Gabrielle picked up her phone and hit a button before tapping her fingers against the desk as she waited. "Hey, April. Priscilla Grant wondered if you had a moment....Hmm, I'm not sure." She put her hand over the mouthpiece and leaned toward Priscilla. "Can you tell me the nature of your visit?"

"I think someone is staying in the...I don't know." Priscilla shrugged helplessly. "It's complicated."

Gabrielle listened a moment, then hung up. "Officer Brown said she'd be right up."

A minute later the officer walked into the reception area. The dark blue uniform of the Tisbury police force was ironed and her shoes polished, and she wore her typical no-nonsense demeanor. "Hello, Priscilla. How can I help?"

"Do you have a place we can talk?" If possible, she didn't want to look like a fool in front of an audience.

"Sure, come on back to the office." April held the door for her, and after they'd entered a small interview room and sat at the table, she focused her attention on Priscilla. "What's going on?"

"I hope you don't think I'm being paranoid."

"I've known you long enough to know your instincts are worth exploring."

"I'm not even sure this qualifies yet, but the questions are nagging me enough to bring in the experts." Priscilla explained about what she had seen and overheard at the garden center. "Then when I came out of the garden center fifteen minutes later, the man was waiting in his car. This is his license plate number." She slid the napkin across the table.

April took it and jotted a note in her pad. "So that's strange, but why come here to tell me about that?"

"Have you heard about *American Antiques* coming to the island Saturday?"

"Yep. Working overtime on Memorial Day weekend thanks to it."

"A friend of my cousin Gail owns a cottage at the campground. She received a postcard from Boston telling her that something valuable was in the cottage, and she asked Gail to go through the cottage to see if she could find anything that would be worth taking to the show. I went with Gail and found a large model ship hidden in a dresser, along with some wooden toys that have since gone missing. Gail's friend claims she's never seen it, but I haven't found any of the renters from last year who say they left it." Priscilla leaned forward. "April, it's too big to simply forget. You'll see what

I mean." She found a photo of it on her phone and held it out for April to view.

"So you think it might be tied to this man somehow?" April's brows arched, and her skepticism was palpable.

"Maybe it's crazy, but I'm wondering if Renee Overman in the association office was telling him when certain cabins would be free, and he either stays in them or hides things in them during the off-season. I know it sounds nuts."

"Or you could be onto something. The question is what." April tapped her pen on the notepad while considering Priscilla. "Let me do some checking for thefts, particularly of small items or antiques. Things like that wouldn't necessarily be immediately obvious in those cabins."

"But whatever he was doing, something went wrong. He was not happy with Renee, and she was scared when I saw her today."

"Do you know her?"

"Not before this week."

"She's relatively new to the island too. At least she didn't grow up here." April looked at her notes. "I can do some poking around and ask her if she's okay. The hard thing is, she has to want help and to tell us what's going on. That isn't always the case."

Priscilla nodded. "I understand, but there was something about that man. He seemed sinister. If he is staying in the cottages or hiding items there, what I can't understand is, why? He wasn't dressed like he was on his last dime. And he's driving a black Audi."

"That's a good point, but it could be more about hiding things." April drew a box around the license plate number. "I have two teenage boys. The hunt is the fun part for them. The flip side is hiding something so well that the other can't find it. Maybe that's what's going on here."

"I don't know about that, but it brings me back to why the ship was in Wanda's cabin. If Renee was letting this man know when the cottages were scheduled to be empty, he might use them to hide things. Then a hiccup happened when Wanda's son rented out the cabin for three or four weeks after the shoulder season without telling Renee."

"Even if that's the case, there was plenty of time later in the winter and this spring to get over there, right?"

"Yes, there should have been." And just like that the theory Priscilla had felt beginning to coalesce fell apart. She sighed and shook her head. "But Renee didn't know we'd be there this week looking for items for the show. Still, I'm not sure it works anyway."

"It was worth exploring." April pushed back from the table. "Anything else?"

"No." Priscilla collected her purse, trying to hide how sheepish she felt. "Sorry to waste your time."

"You didn't. I'll check the license plate number and then talk to Renee once I know the man's name. Be careful, since you inserted yourself into their argument."

"I'm certain he didn't follow me, so I'm not worried." Maybe she should be, she thought, as a flicker of concern darkened April's face. "Besides, I have Jake with me. He'll keep me safe."

April smiled and then stood and straightened her uniform shirt. "I'll call if I learn anything helpful."

"Thanks again for your time."

"Sure thing." April led Priscilla back to the front of the office, then slipped away.

Priscilla told Gabrielle goodbye and hurried to her car. Jake was still sleeping, but his ears pricked up as if he'd heard her steps. A moment later he was wriggling on her lap with happy puppy kisses.

If only solving the mystery of the ship could be as easy as making her dog excited to see her.

CHAPTER EIGHTEEN

As she pulled into the drive leading to her cottage, Priscilla's phone rang. She pulled to a stop and took the call.

"Priscilla, this is Shondra Johnson. We spoke last night."

"Of course. Do you have any information?"

"I might. It's hard to tell with just photos, but I've heard of an item like this. It was part of a private collection in the greater Boston area. They were bidding out for appraisals for insurance purposes. I didn't get the bid, so I didn't see the actual items, but it sounds like one of the unique items they had listed in the request for proposals."

"Is there someone I could follow up with?"

"They're a well-known family that values their privacy, so I don't feel I can give you their information, but I could contact them for you."

Priscilla's thoughts ran as she evaluated the offer. "It's not my ship, so I'll have to check with my friend."

"That's fine. I leave on vacation for the holiday weekend tomorrow. Just let me know before that or after Tuesday."

"All right. Thanks for calling back." Priscilla hung up and considered what to tell Wanda. What did she really know that she could communicate? That Renee might be using her cottage in the off-season, or letting someone who was unauthorized do that?

And there was something about Shondra's offer that made her wonder what strings would be attached to the help. If that family had owned the ship, then there was a bigger issue. The item hadn't been left—it had originally been stolen. She'd feel much better if she could talk to the family directly, though if they were as well known as Shondra indicated, they'd want to keep knowledge of any thefts limited to as few people as possible.

Regardless, she should mention the possibility to April Brown and let her see what she could learn. Maybe the item had never left the island. She called the police department and asked for Officer Brown.

"You just left," Gabrielle groused good-naturedly but patched her through.

April was all business when she got on the phone. "I don't have anything yet."

"I didn't expect you to, but I may have something for you." Priscilla briefly explained about Shondra's call. "I don't know if the ship is from this family or not. I haven't decided whether to ask Wanda about that, but what if people are committing thefts and then leaving the stolen items in the cottages over the off-season? Then they come back to collect them before people return."

"It's possible, but we haven't had a rash of thefts reported."

"But it's possible?"

"Certainly. The items may have been stolen from vacant homes. It's been the off-season and quiet. A smart time to hit the summer homes."

"And rather than move the goods immediately off the island, let the dust settle." Priscilla considered the idea. The man would not have been so threatening to Renee without good reason. "It might be a terrible idea, but I wanted to pass it along."

"I'll see what I can learn."

After they disconnected, Priscilla took Jake for a walk and considered next steps. She'd really like to know for sure whether one of the renters had left the item, but that was beginning to feel unlikely. How was she supposed to know if they never got back to her? Maybe she should take the lack of response as an answer.

When she got back to her cottage, she dialed Wanda's number. Instead of Wanda, a familiar male voice answered. Priscilla frowned and hesitated. "Is Wanda available?"

"Who's calling?"

"Sorry. This is Priscilla Grant, and I need to ask her a question about the cottage."

The man blew out a breath that could have been a snort. "This is her son, Jerry. You're still working on that?"

Priscilla glanced at the clock. It was two o'clock, so she had some time. "I'd really like to come talk to you about it. I can be there in half an hour. Does that work?"

"Sure. I'm here helping Mom with some details around the house. Changing light bulbs and things like that while checking on her post-surgery. I'm staying for dinner before heading back to the city."

"I'll head out shortly."

She gathered her purse and keys, made sure Jake had water, and left the house. Maybe Jerry Shire could help her sort out the timetable of renters and give her some insight on his mother's state of mind.

Jake stared out the front window as she climbed in her car and drove away. She forced her thoughts away from him and in other directions as she made the drive to Wanda's. He'd already been out for a car ride and would be fine at the house.

Would the ship reveal its secrets? Or was it destined to remain a mystery?

When Priscilla arrived at Wanda's, a tall middle-aged man opened the front door and introduced himself as Jerry. "Come on back to the kitchen. Mom is resting, but I thought you could tell me more about the ship, and we can go from there."

Priscilla followed him through the hallway lined with framed photos of the beach in various seasons and weather. The frames matched in size, but the photos were a beautiful hodgepodge. When they reached the kitchen she pointed back toward the hallway and asked, "Did your mom take those photos?"

"No. Most are by my dad, and a few were taken by me. I thought I'd be a photojournalist when I was in college, and then I realized newspapers and most magazines weren't looking for artistic shots. Those that do have more submissions than they can use." He shrugged. "I decided it could be a hobby. I don't do digital photography. I enjoy the process of swishing film and paper through chemicals and watching the image appear. It always seems like magic to me."

"I can imagine. Did you recognize the ship from the pictures I sent you?"

He shook his head. "I have no idea what it was doing in Mom's cottage. I'm sure I'd remember it if I'd seen it."

"And you're sure it wasn't there in December?"

"Sure as I can be, but I didn't stay in that room, and my boys didn't remember anything about it when I asked them." He cocked his head. "I think they would have mentioned it, but I can't be certain."

"That's been the story of this ship. I could be spending all this time trying to return a toy that nobody wants. If they did, they'd return my call or reach out to your mom. Have you ever met Renee Overman?"

"The woman who helps Mom with the cottage?"

"That's the one."

"I've heard Mom talk about her, but I'm not sure I've met her. I don't need to stop by the association office to get a key for the house."

"Well, I saw her today, and she was being cornered by a man who seemed to be talking about the cabins. He was really unhappy about something that had happened."

"That's pretty vague."

"It is. But it made me wonder if the cottages were being used in the off-season without permission."

"By who? The Mafia?"

"I don't know. Maybe."

"You know how that sounds, right?"

Priscilla took a breath and let the silence stretch. "What if someone is hiding himself and/or things in the cabins when no one is checking on them? What if Renee is letting him? That could be how the ship got into the cabin."

"Then you don't have to worry about finding the owner. They left it there without permission, so finders keepers kicks in." He gestured between them. "You found it, so we'll keep it."

"Except he was not happy to find something gone." She crossed her arms to keep from shivering against a sudden chill. "It could be any number of things, but what if it's the ship?"

"The odds of that seem minuscule." He turned toward the sink. "Can I get you something to drink? Water or iced tea? Mom always has some of that in the fridge."

"I always have what?"

Priscilla turned to find Wanda filling the doorway in her wheelchair. Her hair stood up on one side as if it had been flattened against a pillow. "Good afternoon, Wanda."

"Hello to you too." She tipped her head toward her son with a quizzical look. "I lay down for a few minutes, and you start entertaining guests." She waved her hands in the air. "Am I invited to this shindig?"

"It's your house, Mom."

"Glad to hear you say that." She winked at Priscilla. "Jerry likes to take good care of me, but sometimes I'm glad to hear he remembers the house is still mine. Growing old is for the birds."

Jerry shook his head with his lips pressed together as if he was muzzling his thoughts. "Mom, you're barely eighty. You'll be around a long time."

"You'd better hope so." She grinned at Priscilla. "Did the ship bring you back?"

"It did." Priscilla took the glass of iced tea Jerry held out to her and sat at the kitchen table. "I showed Jerry pictures of it, but I'm about to give up on finding where it belongs."

"I really don't want it. I just want something to take to the show. It's too big for my decorating style."

"We can always put it back in the cottage, Mom."

"Then someone will break it. It's big and delicate enough to be a problem." Wanda considered it and then shook her head. "It would be broken by the end of the summer. Whatever it is, it's remarkably intact, and I'd like to keep it that way, even if I don't want it in my house."

Priscilla rubbed her eyes and sagged in her chair. "What do you want me to do with it?"

"I suppose you can leave it here." Wanda frowned. "Do you have a shrink ray? Something to get it down to size?"

"That would make it the size of a Matchbox car, Mom."

"So it would." Wanda tapped the table, then pointed a finger at Priscilla. "What I want to know is, are you going to call the police?"

CHAPTER NINETEEN

All kinds of thoughts collided as Priscilla studied the table's scarred surface. "How much did you hear of what I told Jerry?"

"Enough to know you have a theory."

"It's exactly that. A theory. I can't prove that someone is using the cottages during the off-season to hide things."

Wanda looked at Jerry. "What do you think of this idea?"

"I just heard it." Jerry crossed his arms and leaned against the counter. "It's an interesting one. Kind of out there though." He seemed to dismiss it. "Why would anyone bring things all the way out here? And it's quite a risk to think none of the owners would discover the uninvited use."

Priscilla shook her head. "Not when you realize you hadn't checked the Relic in months. And I don't think you're unique. After your last guest left in October, did anyone spend time there other than over Christmas?"

Wanda shrugged. "No."

"I imagine many of the other owners are similarly hands off." Jerry tapped his phone. "The camp has always been a summer facility. Lots to do then, but a ghost town during the rest of the year."

"There might be one or two cottages in use in the off-season, but most aren't prepared to be used in all seasons." Wanda studied Priscilla. "I looked into refurbishing the cottage with more insulation and other changes one year, but it was going to take much more than I could afford. It made more sense to invest the money here where I live." She glanced around with a twinkle in her eyes. "And clearly, I didn't invest much here."

"So it's reasonable to think that while your cottage was empty over the winter, so were many of the others. It makes the campground an accommodating place to hide valuable items. I talked to the police about the theory, but I don't know what they'll do with it."

"If they don't figure it out, you will."

"What does that mean, Mom?" Jerry looked between the two of them, brows arched.

"Gail told me that Priscilla here is good at solving mysteries. She's developed something of a reputation since she moved to the island." Wanda pushed her wheelchair around. "I'd really like some iced tea. Can you get it for me, Jerry?"

He nodded, and a minute later handed her a tall glass.

She accepted it with thanks. "The question is, what can we do about your theory, Priscilla?"

"Nothing, Mom." Jerry jumped in before Priscilla could begin to form an answer. "You are not going to get involved in some harebrained scheme to decide whether someone is using your summer house. In fact, maybe it's time to get rid of it. We can sell it." Jerry watched his mom closely as if to gauge her reaction, then he continued with enthusiasm. "Yes. That's what we should do. Then it doesn't matter what happens, you don't have to be concerned. It's someone else's problem."

"Maybe I don't want to sell." Wanda's words were heavy with frustration. It sounded as though this wasn't the first time they'd had this conversation. "Nothing has changed, Jerry. The cottage has been in our family for generations, and I'm not selling it. That's the end of the discussion. After all, I'm not the sole owner."

"No, you're just the one who has to do all the work." His tone was disgruntled.

"Which is why I have Renee Overman. She handles most of the details."

As Priscilla listened to the back and forth, she was struck again by how much Wanda relied on others to help her with the cottage. It made sense that at her age, she wouldn't want to run over on a moment's notice, but the Relic was clearly important to her. At the same time, Jerry's posture and frown indicated how frustrated he was with his mother. Why wasn't he willing to help her with something that mattered to her?

Jerry picked up the ice tea pitcher and offered it to Priscilla. "Would you like more?"

"Thank you." Priscilla reached for the pitcher.

Wanda watched as she filled the glass, then set the pitcher down. "Back in the old days, I was a waitress at several of the restaurants on the island." Jerry groaned, and Wanda looked at him. "Son, your father and I worked hard for everything we have.

Maybe that's why I'm not willing to simply sell a portion of our family inheritance. A good job is nothing to be ashamed of."

"You could have been more. Done more."

"I was, and am, content here. This island is my home."

As she listened, Priscilla sensed this was another argument they'd had many times. "The other thing I needed to ask was whether you'd like me to have an antiques appraiser contact a family on your behalf about the ship. She's thinking it might have been stolen from them."

Wanda frowned at her. "Why can't we contact them ourselves?"

"The appraiser is reluctant to give us the family's name. She's concerned it would be a breach of their privacy to hand their information directly to us."

"So instead, she'll give them ours?" Wanda snorted. "I think that's a breach in our direction."

Priscilla glanced at Jerry and was surprised to see that his face had leeched of color. "Are you all right?"

He shook himself as if snapping out of something. "Yeah. Why does she think contacting them would help?"

"This particular family sent out a request for bids for an updated appraisal of their collection. She thought this ship might be part of it." Priscilla raised a hand to stave off questions. "That's all I know."

"Then I'm not willing to share the ship with them." Wanda's jaw firmed, and she looked like a toddler who wouldn't budge.

"All right." Priscilla stood and moved toward the hallway. "Thanks for letting me come. I'll let you get back to your afternoon plans."

Wanda nodded but didn't say anything. It was clear her thoughts were already directed somewhere else. Jerry followed Priscilla to the door.

"Sorry we aren't more help." He opened the door for her. "I'd be happy to keep the ship, so it's not cluttering your house."

She studied him a moment as she tried to discern why he offered. "I don't mind keeping it. Will you be back here on Saturday?"

"Not planning on it. Why?"

"Your mom is set on taking something to the *American Antiques* event. So far that's the ship."

"It won't really matter if she takes anything. She'll probably forget between now and then anyway."

"Actually, I've seen nothing to indicate your mom is anything but on top of things. She's delightful, Jerry."

"She is." He shoved his hands in his pockets. "But you shouldn't be burdened by her latest fascination."

"I'm not." She smiled brightly at him. "Any word on your friend who used the cottage?"

"No. I would have mentioned it if there was."

"What was his name again? Anthony? Reeding?"

"No. Adam Reeling." The last name sounded mumbled, but she was past asking again.

"Well, I'll let your mom know if I learn anything else." Priscilla started through the door, but not before he grabbed her arm.

"Be careful." He loosened his grip as if realizing he'd held on harder than he intended. "You're a nice lady, and I don't want you to get hurt."

She shook free of his hold. "What do you mean?"

"Just be careful." He turned and closed the door, leaving Priscilla staring at it.

She shook herself and headed to her car. While there were odd things about her interactions with Jerry, she wasn't sure what they meant. She needed a brisk walk with Jake on the shoreline to clear her head and help her think more clearly.

She drove up her driveway and parked the car. She was juggling her keys out of her purse when she noticed that the front door was cracked open. There was no car in the driveway or in view, and no one was in sight. She held her breath, her heart hammering, and listened for any sound coming from inside the house. Nothing. Where was Jake?

She checked her watch and decided to try Gerald. He said he'd be home sometime today. With shaking hands, she tugged her phone from her pocket and hit her speed dial.

"Good afternoon, sunshine."

"Are you back in town?"

"Just got here. Why?"

"I just got home and my front door is cracked open." She rubbed her arm. "I didn't leave it that way."

"Get back in your car and lock the doors. I'm on my way now."

"I have to find Jake."

"Not if it means you're in danger." She heard his car start. "I'll help you find him when I get there."

"All right." But it didn't mean she had to stay in her driveway like a sitting duck for whoever might be out there. She got in her car and backed to the end of the driveway. At moments like this she wished she had a long winding driveway. Instead it was a short drive from the road to the house. Mature trees to the north of the cottage kept it fairly sheltered from neighbors. Add the thin spit of beach down the steps from the yard, and she was fairly isolated.

Time crawled by as she waited for Gerald to show up.

She scanned her yard and the path near the lighthouse looking for Jake. His brown and white fur didn't show up as far as she could see. Hopefully that meant he was still inside and hadn't escaped. Or been hurt.

Searching for him would be a terrible end to a not so great day.

Finally, she heard Gerald's car behind hers. She glanced at her dashboard clock. She'd only waited minutes. She pulled forward in front of the house and parked, and he followed her, then hopped out of his vehicle. She rolled down her car window, and he leaned down into it.

"You okay?"

"Yes. I'm probably just being paranoid."

"Better safe." He met her gaze with his steady one. "You're not someone who overreacts, Priscilla. If you feel uncomfortable, then that's enough for me." He stood up and glanced around, then opened her door. "I don't like you being out here, outside of town, by yourself."

"I have been for two years, Gerald. It's fine."

"We'll see." He helped her out of the vehicle, then closed the door. "Go ahead and lock it."

She did, and they walked to the house. The door eased open with barely a touch. Inside the couch cushions were on the floor and bookshelves swept clean.

Priscilla took a deep breath, and Gerald pushed her behind him. "Stay here."

"Why would someone do this?" She scanned the mess, but didn't hear Jake's toenails against the floor. "Where's Jake?"

"We'll find him." Gerald understood her fierce love for her dog. "Keep your eyes open for anything that's missing."

"I'm not sure I'd notice in this mess. Should I call the police?"

"Yes, but stay close."

She dialed 911 while staying glued to Gerald's side as they walked through her home, confirming no one lurked in a corner. Dispatch assured her they'd send someone. As they waited, they walked around the yard calling Jake's name, checking under bushes in case he was injured.

"Did you notice anything missing?"

"Other than Jake?" Priscilla shook her head as the breeze pushed her hair into her face. "Why would someone break into my cottage? Anything of value would be in the lighthouse." She straightened up from looking under a shrub. "We haven't looked down by the lighthouse. Maybe Jake is there."

"Let's check it out."

When they walked around the house toward the lighthouse, Priscilla noticed how the tower's crisp white paint glowed in the sunlight, and the black railing crowned the lighthouse. While all looked as it should, she felt unsettled. They checked inside, and she was relieved to discover that nothing seemed disturbed or missing. But there was still no sign of Jake. They came back outside when they heard a car pull up.

CHAPTER TWENTY

Captain Hank Weston stepped from his squad car and strode toward her, his size emphasized by his uniform. He shook Gerald's hand and then turned to Priscilla. "Sounds like you've had a full day, Priscilla." His words were colored slightly by his thick local accent.

"I didn't expect it to end this way."

"No one does. Why don't you tell me what's happened?"

As they walked to the front door, she filled him in on arriving home to find the door partially opened, and then calling Gerald for help.

"Did you go inside?"

"Yes."

"Priscilla." He drew her name out until it had several extra syllables.

"We didn't touch anything, though I would love to start cleaning."

"Was anything damaged?"

"Not that we could tell, but they made quite a mess in the living room." She thought about it a moment. "In fact, that might be the only room the intruder entered. The others look fine, like maybe someone walked through them but not much more."

Chief Westin pulled out his phone. "Let me call for the crime scene team."

"Is that really necessary?" The thought of more people crawling all over her house made Priscilla feel almost as queasy as knowing someone had forcefully invaded it earlier. One look from Chief Westin had her backtracking. "Silly question. Of course it's necessary." She knew she was babbling. "I don't suppose it comes with a cleaning service."

"Not on our budget." He placed the call and then turned to Gerald. "This might be a good time to take her to dinner. Get her away from here while we do our work."

"For the record, I'm standing right here."

The men exchanged knowing looks.

"Where would you like to go, Priscilla?"

Priscilla looked at him, her eyes filling with tears. "Gerald, I can't go anywhere without knowing what's happened to Jake. I have to find him—he could be hurt."

Gerald gave her a side hug. "We'll find him, sweetheart. I know if it were Sammy, I'd be frantic."

She grabbed Jake's leash and a bag of treats, hoping Gerald was right. They went outside and left the police to do their job in the house.

As Priscilla and Gerald walked the beach, her thoughts were on one thing. She needed to find her pooch.

"He's out here somewhere, Priscilla. We'll find him."

"I'm sure." She sighed as she made her way down the stairs. They were still solid, something that she gauged every month or so. The salt in the air could make the wood deteriorate more quickly than usual.

The beach felt calm, quiet.

Her heart sank. If Jake were on the beach, he'd be dashing from one thing to the next, sniffing for anything interesting. The last time he'd gotten free, she'd waited on the bottom step until he wore down and came and flopped down next to her. Now she wished she'd see him out zig-zagging on the narrow spit of land.

"Let's head toward town. He probably kept going down the beach." Gerald took her hand, and she let him lead her that direction even as she wondered if Jake had gone the opposite direction.

They walked farther down the beach, calling Jake's name. The stretch of beach narrowed before it widened a bit on the way into Vineyard Haven. The beach around Martha's Vineyard wasn't a typical sand beach for most of the island. Instead it was a thin strip of sand and rock between the ocean and the land that supported the sea grasses and homes. A cluster of rocks sat near the waves...and around them circled a brown and white speckled animal.

"There he is!" Priscilla dropped Gerald's hand and hurried toward the rocks. "Jake! Jake, come here."

The terrier lifted his head, and then froze. Would he bolt, or come? "Don't run, boy."

Jake sank to his haunches and waited. Maybe he'd decided it was time for food and water.

Gerald laughed. "Someone knows which side his bread is buttered on."

"Small favors." Priscilla closed the remaining distance and clipped the leash on Jake's collar. "There." The weight of her concern for him drained away, and she felt limp. "Let's get you back home."

As they neared the stairs, Gerald paused. "How can I help? Want me to help you clean up? Oh, I brought the ship back. I do have something interesting to tell you that I learned in Provincetown about it."

Jake skipped up the stairs, pulling Priscilla after him. Oh, to have his boundless reserves of energy. "I would appreciate the help, Gerald. I won't be able to think about anything until things are put right. But I'm sure the police aren't done with their search yet."

Gerald extended his hand. "You might as well make the most of the situation. How about I take you to dinner?" He grinned. "There are worse ways to spend an evening."

"Dinner sounds nice." She smiled back at him. "Let's let the chief know we found Jake."

She gave the good news to Chief Weston and shut Jake up in her bedroom. "See if you can stay out of trouble till I get back." She wagged her finger at him, then bent and kissed his furry head.

She turned back to Gerald. "Let's grab a sandwich at Candy's and then head to the Boardwalk for ice cream. I heard they're trying out new flavors in anticipation of the tourists returning. I've been hungry for a Blitz." The confection of graham-cracker-flavored ice cream with chocolate chunks and ribbons of caramel was a sweet delight.

"Or we could go straight to dessert." Gerald's hazel eyes twinkled as he led her to his vehicle and opened the passenger door.

"I've always thought dessert should be the first course, but that might not be the healthiest choice."

"It won't hurt anything just this once." Gerald drove them into town, and Priscilla tried to simply enjoy the moment. She was riding with her favorite man to get a sweet treat. When she got home, she'd deal with the mess in her living room.

Gerald parked in front of the boardwalk and helped her from the car. He stopped before they reached the door. "Do you want to claim one of the picnic tables, and I'll get our ice cream?"

Only a couple of the dozen tables were open, so she nodded. "I can do that."

With the sun beginning to slide behind buildings, the evening was promising to be a perfect one for eating ice cream outside. She enjoyed watching people walk by as she waited for Gerald. When she considered how many people would love to live on the island but couldn't afford it, she was grateful to think she'd had the opportunity to settle there.

"Fancy seeing you here." Mildred sank onto the bench across from her. Her Revolutionary War-style bonnet sat askew on her hair, the bun at the nape of her neck slipping to the side. She blew out a breath and leaned toward Priscilla. "What a day. I felt sure it would never end."

"Why's that?"

"There was a visit from the *American Antiques* producer, Anna something or other. There are a lot of things they forgot to tell me, so I have to figure out how to get them ready for Saturday."

"Like what?"

"A second stable power source. I'm not even sure what that is."

"Maybe Gerald or someone else can help."

"Maybe, but he shouldn't have to." She glanced up. "Speaking of the man, there he is. Did you two skip straight to dessert?"

Gerald held up one of the dishes. "Your Boardwalk Blitz, madam. And we did. We aren't getting any younger, so we decided to enjoy every bit of this life."

"Thank you." Priscilla accepted the dish and took a bite, letting the sweetness sit on her tongue before swallowing. "Gerald, Mildred needs a second stable power source at the museum. Any ideas?"

"Sure. We have extra generators at the Coast Guard station for use in storms. I bet you could borrow a couple of those." He took a quick bite of his double-chocolate cone. "I might know someone who could help arrange that for you."

Mildred nodded, and a hint of a smile played on her lips as her shoulders relaxed. "That would be a relief. I'll admit when they mentioned that requirement, I about panicked. Even if I understood what they were talking about, finding it in two days could be crazy." She pushed to her feet and straightened her bonnet. "Well, I'll get my chocolate shake and let you lovebirds enjoy your dessert in silence."

"You can join us, Mildred." Priscilla looked at Gerald, who nodded.

"We're just killing time until we can go back into Priscilla's house."

Mildred's eyebrows arched. "Why can't you go in the house?"

Priscilla wanted to skewer Gerald with a glance. He didn't need to bring it up. "Someone broke into the cottage while I was out this afternoon. Chief Westin called out a crime scene unit of some sort to take photos and fingerprints."

Mildred shook her head. "There's always something exciting happening around you, Priscilla."

"That's one way of putting it." Priscilla took another bite of her ice cream. "Everything else coming together for Saturday?"

"Sure, sure." Mildred's shoulders sagged further, and she looked less than convincing. "I'll be glad when Saturday is behind us. It's a great idea in theory to host the show, but it's also overwhelming to think of a television crew parked in my museum for an entire day and a half. They'll start setting up Friday. It's going to be chaos."

"For a good cause." Priscilla reached across the table. "Just think of the free publicity for the museum."

"That's what I keep telling myself, but I'm not sure it's worth the added stress. I guess we'll find out when the episode airs." She patted the top of the picnic table. "Well, kids, I'm getting my shake. See you later."

Priscilla watched Mildred enter the ice cream shop. "She seems worn out."

"I imagine getting ready for the media will do that, especially when she isn't used to them." Gerald took another bite of his ice cream.

A vaguely familiar voice behind them caused Priscilla to glance over her shoulder. Renee sat at a table a few feet away. She was talking into a phone but was keeping her words quiet enough to provide only a murmur in the background. Then she was quiet a minute as if listening to someone.

Gerald followed her gaze. "Who is that?"

"Renee Overman. Do you know her?"

He scrutinized her a minute, and Priscilla almost kicked him under the table to break his focus. "No."

"She works at the camp meeting association."

"And you're concerned about her."

"A bit. She hasn't been completely honest with me or with Wanda Shire about who she's allowed to use Wanda's family cottage. I saw her at the garden center this morning, and a man was there, cornering her. It seemed like he was threatening her, so I interrupted them."

"Next time call for help. Don't insert yourself into it." Gerald's tone was deadly serious.

"I don't always have time to send out an SOS, Gerald. Sometimes I have to act based on the best information I have at the time. It felt like something bad was going to happen if I didn't intervene."

Gerald focused his attention on the remains of his ice cream. She knew that meant he was focusing his thoughts on how to reply. He took the last bite and then looked at her. "Priscilla, I care too much to let you race into every situation without asking you to be careful." There was sweet intensity to his words.

"He's coming after me. I don't know what he's going to do, but I'm scared."

Renee's voice rose, and Priscilla glanced at Gerald. He shook his head and then stood. "Let's go see what she needs."

When Priscilla stepped in front of Renee, the woman startled and hurried to get off the phone. "I'll call you back." She slipped her phone in her purse, looking between Priscilla and Gerald. "Can I help you?"

"We couldn't help overhearing your conversation." Priscilla tried to stay relaxed and nonthreatening, but Renee looked anything but relaxed. "Are you okay?"

"I was until you decided to stick your nose into my morning. I was fine at the garden center."

"You didn't look fine."

"Well, appearances don't always represent reality. Now I have a highly irate client and no way to explain to him why our transaction was interrupted this morning."

"But why are you scared?" Priscilla wasn't sure how best to defuse Renee's animosity, but Gerard didn't say anything until she glanced at him.

"If you're afraid, I can possibly arrange protection for you."

"That's exactly what I need. Some Coasties looking over my shoulder and following my every move. No thanks." She huffed to her feet.

Priscilla held her hands in front of her as if to calm a scared child. "Let us help you, Renee."

"I don't need your help."

"Do you want to know my theory? About what's happening with the cottages?"

"I'm not interested in fiction." Renee pushed past them. "Now, if you'll let me go, I have things I need to do." She walked to her car and drove off in a spray of gravel.

Priscilla rubbed her face with her hands, feeling the sugar spike from her ice cream fade away. "Do you think we can head home?"

"Yes, we should do that. I'd like to take another walk on the beach."

It was such a narrow strip near her home. Large rocks held back the waves and erosion, leaving only a thin slice of sand and gravel to walk, but there was still something incredibly peaceful about walking it. The crash of waves and cawing of seagulls provided a soundtrack that filled her with peace. Walking that spit of land with Gerald only made it more meaningful.

"That would be nice. You can tell me what you learned in Provincetown."

When they returned to the cottage and lighthouse, no cars waited in the driveway.

"Let's get Jake," Priscilla said. They went in the house, and she opened her bedroom door. Jake ran to his water bowl. He slurped up water in frenzied gulps that left water splashing outside the bowl.

"That is quite the mess, boy." She'd need to find a towel to clean it up, but before she turned around Gerald already had one and was crouching next to her dog.

"We need to teach you some drinking manners." After a few swipes, he ruffled the dog's fur and stood. Priscilla brought Jake's leash and snapped it on his collar.

She was quiet as they walked, and Gerald let the silence stretch as they strolled. Her mind was full as she thought about the week. She'd been to the campground so many times, but was still no closer to understanding the ship or what was going on with it. She needed to turn some of her attention to getting ready for Hugh and Marigold's wedding so she could honor them in their moment. She'd bought all those plants earlier and didn't know when she'd have the time to do anything with them.

With *American Antiques* only two days away, she didn't have much more time to try to figure out the ship's value or who it belonged to. So far her efforts hadn't led to too many fruitful places. She sighed, and Gerald took her hand. He tugged her to a stop. "Priscilla."

She turned toward him, and he took both her hands in his, slowing her feet and quickening her heart rate.

He touched his forehead to hers. "Priscilla, I know you. There are a million thoughts racing through your brain right now, aren't there?"

She sighed and leaned into him. She felt tears behind her eyes. Frustrated tears, worried tears, relieved tears, happy tears. How could a person feel so many emotions at once?

Gerald squeezed her hands, then wrapped his arms tightly around her. Her tears fell faster, and she burrowed into his shoulder, drawing peace from his strength and love.

When she'd cried herself out, he loosened his hold, cupped her face between his warm, calloused hands, and wiped the tears from her cheeks. When he spoke, his voice was low, and shaky. "When you told me your house had been broken into, it scared me to death. What if the intruder was still there? What if he wanted to harm you? I don't want to let go of you, Priscilla."

They clung to each other until Jake gave a sharp bark and tugged on his leash.

Priscilla laughed and pulled back. "Our chaperone is bored."

Gerald chuckled and linked arms with her, turning back toward the cottage. "Then we better get back before curfew."

"Is the ship in your car?" Priscilla asked when they got to the house.

"It is. I'll get it while you get us something to drink. Sound good?"

"Yup. Iced tea okay?"

"It's fine." He disappeared, and she took Jake into the house. After getting the leash off him, she went to the kitchen and pulled out the glasses and pitcher of tea.

Gerald appeared in the kitchen doorway holding the ship. He put it on the small kitchen counter. "I left your box and packing material in the living room."

"Do you think the ship is safe sitting there?"

"I'm not planning on knocking it off. Are you?"

"No." She smiled as she handed him a glass of tea. "I'm ready to hear what you found out in Provincetown."

"And I'm ready to tell you. It's not something that will help you in your quest for information about this particular ship, but nevertheless, it is interesting. One of the captains I met during the inspection collects Coast Guard model ships, and has one of a lightship, the *Nantucket*, I think he said. He's researched quite a bit about them. He said they were also used in heavy fog, when the visibility fell below one and a half miles. Sometimes the vapor would be so dense during a subzero winter night, the only part of the ship that would be visible was the top of the masts."

"So the lightship had a foghorn, just like a lighthouse?"

"It did, yes. And if the foghorn for some reason wouldn't work, the men had to ring a bell by hand, taking fifteen-minute shifts because of the frigid subzero weather. It was not a job for the fainthearted." He paused. "There's something else."

He picked up the ship and shook it. Priscilla heard a faint rattling sound.

"What was that?"

"I don't know." Gerald shook it again, and the noise repeated. "Chickie and I discovered that noise when we took it out of the box."

Priscilla groaned. "I hope I didn't break it. It hasn't made that sound before. I thought I wrapped it up well enough."

"You're a pretty careful person. I doubt you did anything to it."

Priscilla ran her hands along the sides of the ship.

"What are you doing?"

"Looking for a way to open it. If it's something that was added, it had to get in there somehow."

"I hope you have better luck than Chickie and I did. We tried for a long time and never figured out any way to open it. The only thing we can figure is that whoever made the model put something in there and glued it shut."

"It would be a good place to hide something small. And a ship wouldn't be as obviously out of place in a seaside cabin as something else might be."

"Like an antique Chinese vase." Gerald looked at her with a twinkle in his eyes.

"Exactly. The nautical theme is more like what you'd expect to find in a vacation cabin." She scanned the top of the ship. There was nothing on the deck that looked like an opening. No stairs to the inside. "I just don't see where something could have been inserted."

"If the ship isn't valuable, then whoever slipped something in there wouldn't necessarily care about destroying it to get whatever it was out." He shrugged. "I'll have to think about it some more, but whatever is in there right now, I don't see how to get it out."

"It would make a great way to hide something," she repeated.

"Yes. The question is what?"

"Something small, like jewelry."

"Or drugs."

Priscilla looked at him with wide eyes. "Really?"

"Coast Guard. We spend a lot of time searching for drugs. Hiding drugs in empty cottages until the season hits makes a lot of sense."

"It would be worth breaking into my house to find."

"Yes, it could be, though I would have expected a heavier search."

Priscilla shook her head. "Unless they didn't think we'd realize there was something in the ship, which was true until you brought it in. It doesn't sound like there's much in there."

"It's just a theory. It could be a priceless necklace."

"Or nothing at all." If only they could get inside the ship without destroying it. She sighed and sank into a chair. Staring at the ship wasn't going to make a magical portal to the inside suddenly appear.

"Before I leave, can you confirm with Chief Westin that he doesn't have any concerns about you staying tonight?" Gerald's words snapped her from her thoughts, and she nodded.

"I was just thinking the same thing." She knew it had to be safe to be in her home or he wouldn't have let her come back, but as she looked into the living room at the chaos that needed to be cleaned and straightened, it was a stark reminder that her home had been invaded.

The chief answered on the second ring. "Priscilla, you back home?"

"I am. Is that okay?"

"Yes. We didn't find anything that indicated who broke in. Took a few fingerprints and will run them through the system, but that's not as quick as they make it look on TV. The officer tried to clean up as she went."

"She did." It wasn't terribly noticeable which surfaces the fingerprints had been taken from. "Can I start putting things away?"

"Sure. Just keep your doors locked. I don't think you're in danger, but without knowing why someone broke in..." His words trailed off.

"I understand. I haven't found anything missing yet but haven't been inside long."

"I can have the patrol officer drive by a couple times tonight if that makes you feel more comfortable."

While it might, it also seemed like a waste of police resources. "You don't need to do that. If I get that uncomfortable, I'll go stay with Joan or Trudy." Her gaze traveled over the books strewn about the floor, and she sighed. "Chief, do you have one more minute?"

"Sure."

"Did Officer Brown talk to you about my idea of local cottages being used to hide stolen items during the off-season?"

"She did. I know she's started asking some questions, but we haven't received reports of burglaries. Nothing out of the ordinary anyway."

"But the season's only starting."

"True. Which means we may start getting reports as people return to the island. She's also checking with departments on the mainland to see if there's anything that's been happening there we should know about. It's possible that someone is moving things from the mainland to the island, but then they have to move it off again. Unless they're stealing items that would be highly recognizable when fenced, it seems like an extra step that adds to the danger of being caught."

She'd had similar thoughts. "Thanks for letting her check."

"It's been a quiet week, so she's had some time. But can you explain why you asked?"

She filled the chief in on the ship and her search. "I'm not sure it'll lead anywhere, but it's definitely made me ask some questions."

"Keep us posted."

"Will do. Thank you for your help." She hung up and looked at Gerald. "I'm good to stay here."

"Lock the door behind me, and don't let anyone in after me."

"Yes sir." She saluted, then turned serious. "Gerald, I've lived here by myself for almost two years. I know how to do it and be safe."

"True, but you don't often have people breaking in. Let me help you get this room set to rights."

They spent the next fifteen minutes getting books back on shelves and the cushions on the couch the correct way. She could organize the bookshelves later, but it helped to not have her literary friends cast about on the floor.

Gerald didn't seem eager to leave, and she appreciated his company. Then his cell beeped with a text.

"Looks like they need me to come check on something at the station." Gerald kissed her cheek as he left. "Be careful."

"I will. Call me?"

He gave her a smoldering look that curled her toes. "Count on it."

She watched him get into his vehicle, and then closed the door. She tugged back the café curtain and waited until his SUV pulled onto the road. Then she turned to Jake, who had followed her to the door. "It feels empty now, doesn't it, boy?"

She let the curtain fall and went back into the kitchen to put the glasses in the sink. Her eyes fell on the model ship again, sitting on the counter at an angle, as if it were plowing through a rough sea.

She shivered as she imagined the bone-chilling cold seeping into every crack, carried by the smothering fog. In her mind she squinted into the blinding whiteness, hardly able to see her hand in front of her face. She saw a crewman struggling to cross the deck, slick from frozen spray, to reach the bell to guide ships lost in the fog. His clothes and hair crusted with ice, his beard white from his own breath.

And then she was staring at the model ship on her counter again, safe in her warm kitchen, jolted by a thought. She was beginning to feel something about this case she'd never felt before. What did it mean, and what could she do about it?

CHAPTER TWENTY-ONE

None of that," she scolded herself. She needed to do something that would get her back on the right track. What could she do that wasn't spinning her thoughts in a constant loop of questions?

Maybe she should press Jerry Shire about Adam Reeling. She picked up her phone and found his number in her recent calls.

He picked up with a grumpy greeting. "Do you know what time it is?"

She glanced at the clock hanging on the wall. "It's nine thirty."

"Most people don't call strangers at that time of night."

She rolled her eyes but tried to keep her voice steady. "I'm sorry this feels late. That wasn't my intent, so I'll keep this quick. Can I get Adam Reeling's phone number from you? I really need to talk to him. I can keep calling you to ask for that information, or you can give it to me now, and we'll be done."

"Why are you so tenacious about this?"

"Because your mom asked for my help, and once I commit to something, I see it through to the end. Something strange is going on with your cabin, and I think Adam can help me narrow the time frame."

"Fine." He rattled off the number. "Anything else, so you don't have to call again?"

"Not that I can think of right now." She paused, searching for the right words to get through to him. "Jerry, you should care about this more than I do. Something your mom doesn't recognize was left in your family's cottage. I've also uncovered that the woman your mom trusts to be a caretaker for the cottage isn't being one hundred percent truthful with her. Why don't you care about this? She could be cheating your mom out of money she earned."

"Do you know that she's withheld money?"

"No, but it's a likely extension of not being honest about who rented the cottage."

"Then let us pursue that. We can ask for an accounting of the books or something similar. That's not something for you to be concerned about." Jerry paused and then continued. "Let me take care of my mom. You focus on the ship."

Priscilla found herself holding a silent phone. She blew out a breath and looked at Jake. "Well, that went well."

Sometime she would ask Jerry why he was so reticent and untrusting, but at least she could call the last person who had stayed in the cottage. She glanced at the clock. It was still before ten, so she entered Adam's number. A moment later he answered.

"Hello? Who is this?"

"Hi, my name is Priscilla Grant, and I'm a friend of Wanda Shire, the woman whose cottage you used on Martha's Vineyard in the fall. The one called Relic?"

"Okay . . . ?"

"Do you have a minute to answer a couple of questions?"

"I suppose." There was a resettling noise as if he was getting more comfortable on a couch or chair. "It was a nice cottage. Is that what you needed to know? Met my needs. Gave me a place to focus. Though the bed could use a new mattress. Felt thin in places."

"I'm sure she'll appreciate knowing that, but I actually wanted to ask you about something that was in the cottage."

"Oh." He was silent a moment, and then his voice was cautious. "I didn't take anything from the cottage."

"We don't think you did. I'm helping Wanda with a project and found something that had been left in the cottage. It's a three-foot model ship. Did you happen to notice it when you were there?"

"Can't say that I did. I was working on my dissertation, and I was pretty focused. Tried to keep my head down and get the work done while I had use of the cottage."

"What's your dissertation on?"

"Molecular chemistry." He paused. "I can go on if you like."

"I'm sure I wouldn't understand if you did. Congratulations on finishing it. I know that's a big accomplishment."

"It felt like it was going to kill me, then Jerry offered the cottage. It's hard to get into the head space where you can focus on the words. I have a hard time concentrating if I have any distractions at all." His voice warmed as if he were thinking of pleasant memories. "Staying in Relic gave me a place to put my head down and work. Did you know there isn't even Wi-Fi at the cottage? I had to go to the library for that."

Priscilla smiled at the way he sounded as if he'd roughed it without that essential service. "What did you think of the cottage?"

"It was enough but not overly equipped. Where was this ship?"

"It was in a chest of drawers in the bedroom with two twin beds."

"Huh. Don't remember that, but I stayed in the room with the larger bed. I gave up twin beds when I was a teen." He chuckled wryly. "I kept growing, but the beds didn't."

Priscilla laughed. "That seems to be the way it works." She paused. "It's possible it may have been somewhere else when you were there."

He paused. "I don't remember it. Sorry I can't be more helpful."

"I appreciate your time. One more thing. Did you pay Wanda or Jerry for the cottage?"

"Neither. Jerry owed me for something else, so it was a good way to clear that debt."

Three weeks at a cottage on the island to pay a debt? Must have been worth at least six or seven thousand dollars, even in the shoulder season. "Sounds like it worked well for both of you."

"Sure did."

Priscilla hung up and considered calling Jerry back. She'd like to probe him on the extravagant gift to his friend, but he probably wouldn't be very open. And perhaps it was as simple a matter as his family having an empty cottage and his friend having a need.

While she might not have much to follow up on there, she needed one more trip to visit Renee Overman.

And Priscilla was looking forward to that probably even less than Renee herself.

Thursday morning, the weather report indicated that it could rain most of the next two days, so Priscilla decided to work on the yard. If she was going to get things ready for Hugh and Marigold's wedding, she needed to mow and plant the flowers and bushes she'd purchased.

The hour went quickly as she worked up a sweat on the mower. Then she turned to the plants where she'd set them against the garage. This was going to take time, but would look wonderful when they were all in the ground.

Digging holes was not her favorite chore, but as she set the plants into their new homes, she loved how it was coming together.

By noon, the sun was disappearing as clouds skated across the sky.

She wiped the sweat from her forehead and leaned the garden tools back in their spot in the garage. Then she circled the yard and took in the fruit of her labor. It was coming together and would be ready for whatever ceremony Hugh and Marigold decided to have. She'd leave it to Gail to tell her what she needed next, but Priscilla was pleased with how the yard looked.

Regardless of how many came to the wedding, she'd enjoy the plants for years.

After cleaning up she called Gerald.

He answered on the first ring. "Hey you."

"Hey yourself. Listen, are you free for a quick lunch?"

"As a matter of fact, I am. Where would you like to go?"

Priscilla thought for a moment. "How about the Colonial?"

"Sounds good. Can I meet you there in about twenty minutes?"

"Absolutely. I can taste the lobster salad already."

Priscilla climbed into her car and headed to the Colonial Inn. When she got there, she saw Gerald's SUV, so she parked and hurried to the restaurant. He was waiting just inside the door for her, and took her coat as Tilly came up to greet them.

"Priscilla, Gerald, good to see some familiar faces. I'm hoping someone can sit in my restaurant and not bore me to tears talking about this antique something or other show that's coming to town. Do you think you two can carry on a normal conversation?"

Priscilla looked at Gerald and saw that he was biting his lip. She smiled at the feisty woman who was more than a bit her senior. "We'll do our best, Tilly."

Tilly looked at her dubiously. "Hmmph. We'll see. It's all anyone is talking about. Don't people have lives anymore?"

She led them, mumbling all the way, to their usual table. She was still mumbling when she left them with menus and signaled their waitress.

Gerald finally blew out his breath and laughed. "One thing about Tilly. You never have to wonder what she's thinking."

They were still laughing when Hilda came to take their orders. Once they'd ordered and had their iced tea, Gerald sat back in his chair. "How's the sleuthing coming? Have you uncovered any more clues?"

Priscilla picked up her fork and tapped it on the table. "I've run into something I haven't encountered before, and I wanted to tell you about it."

"Oh?" Gerald leaned forward, took the fork from her, and then took her hand, squeezing it.

"This is the first time since I started solving cases—way back to the first one when I first got here—that I'm hoping I don't solve the case." There. She'd said it.

Gerald looked just as puzzled as she knew he would. "Why wouldn't you want to solve it?" he asked gently.

She took a deep breath. "I don't want to find out who the ship belongs to, because...because I really hope I can keep it."

Gerald smiled. "I can understand that." He gave her hand another squeeze.

Priscilla looked into his eyes for the first time. "You can?"

"Of course. I'm not surprised at all. It's the reason I knew you'd be so happy to find out what kind of ship it is. Your lighthouse has brought you adventure, new surroundings, and rekindled connections to your family. And the Coast Guard"—he placed his hand dramatically over his heart—"has brought you your one true love." He grinned at her. "How could you not want the ship for yourself?"

Priscilla let out a shaky breath. "Well, when you put it that way...and so modestly, I might add..." She rolled her eyes. "It helps just to say it out loud. I was feeling pretty guilty about it."

Gerald sobered. "You have nothing to feel guilty about, Priscilla. I know you're going to do your best to solve this mystery for Wanda, and you'll let the chips fall where they may. You don't have a selfish bone in your body, no matter what your feelings say."

"Well, I'm not going to try to persuade you out of that opinion," said Priscilla. She looked over Gerald's shoulder. "Uh-oh, here comes Tilly." She raised her voice. "Now Gerald, I don't know how you can think your antique butter dish is worth more than my vintage eggbeater. We'll just have to ask Tilly what she thinks."

Tilly was still sputtering, and they were still laughing, when their meals arrived.

CHAPTER TWENTY-TWO

After appeasing Tilly and sharing an antique-free meal with Gerald, Priscilla drove to the campground. She hoped that by waiting until after lunch, Renee would be more receptive to her visit. When she'd told Gail a few days earlier that she would help her with a quick look around the cottage, she hadn't imagined it would become such a frequent trip for her. At this point her car could probably get there on autopilot.

There were a few more cars in the parking lot with the Martha's Vineyard Camp Meeting Association tags on the dashboards. Probably more arrivals for the holiday weekend checking into the cottages. Hopefully Renee wasn't too busy to answer a few more questions.

Before she got out of her car, Priscilla paused. *Lord, give me the right words to say. She's not going to be excited to see me.*

She had a feeling that was an understatement, based on Renee's reception the last time she'd been in the office. Renee was beginning to dread Priscilla's appearance, not the kind of response Priscilla liked to generate when she arrived somewhere.

The association's office was full, with one couple standing at the desk when Priscilla peeked in the window. She stepped back and took a seat on the steps as she waited. She didn't want to give

Renee the opportunity to slip away. Based on her reaction the last time Priscilla had stopped by, it wasn't out of the question that Renee would sneak out the back door and disappear.

When the couple walked out, the woman had a flamingo key chain dangling from her fingers and a happy smile on her face. "This is going to be an amazing week." She reached up and kissed the man's cheek.

They came down the stairs, and Priscilla stood, feeling their excitement and joy.

Her phone rang, and Priscilla paused to dig it from her bag. "Hello?"

"Hi, Mom." Rachel sounded breathless, like she was in the middle of rushing between activities.

"Hey, sweetie. Everything going okay?" Priscilla walked off the porch into the small yard, putting a little distance between herself and the office.

"Yes. Too well, actually." Rachel sighed but it had a happy tinge to it. "I shared an idea in a meeting yesterday for a client. They liked it."

"That's great!"

"It is, but it means I'll need to put in some time Saturday to implement those great ideas. Then AJ and I already had plans for Monday. I'm sorry, but it won't work for me to come to the island this weekend."

"You have a busy life. I understand. After all, if you were still in Kansas, I wouldn't expect to see you." Priscilla forced a smile into her words even as she felt the weight of disappointment. "I know you'll do a great job and be able to celebrate your success. In fact, we'll do that at Candy's the next time you're on the island."

"Oh, don't tempt me to make a dash."

"Well, it's closed on Sundays, so we'd have to wait until your next visit anyway."

They chatted for a few more minutes as another party brushed past Priscilla into the office. When the call ended, she waited until the new arrival left. Then she took a deep breath and headed back onto the porch. This would go well. She simply needed an answer to one question. Unfortunately, it was a question she suspected Renee would want to avoid.

She opened the door and stepped into the office. The aroma of grapefruit and mint tickled her nose from a lit candle, and there was a tub of ice with water bottles next to the door. The combination was welcoming and warm.

"Help yourself to water, and I'll be right with you." Renee's voice filtered from the back of the cottage.

Priscilla took a bottle and twisted the lid off before taking a sip.

"How can I help you?" Renee's question reached Priscilla before the woman turned the corner. She froze when she spotted Priscilla. "You? Again?" She sighed and sank into her chair, making the desk a barrier between them. "I have nothing to say."

"Then this will be really fast."

"I certainly hope so. As I'm sure you noticed as you walked across the campground, we have a lot of people checking in today." She pulled a calendar in front of her. "That means I don't have time to deal with distractions like you."

"I would just like to double-check the renters' confirmation information you gave me." Priscilla smiled. "I don't want to think it's anything other than an honest mistake, but I find it odd that the only people I can find are the three who called me back. For eleven people from a set of fourteen to not respond to calls or emails doesn't seem like a coincidence."

"People are busy."

"Maybe. But not all of them."

Renee rolled her eyes. "I don't have anything to say."

"Then just show me where the file with their information is. I haven't gotten Wanda involved yet, because I don't want to damage your relationship with her, but we need to figure this out."

Renee stiffened. "Is that a threat?"

"No. But I'll have to tell her what I've learned eventually."

Renee changed tack. "Why does it matter if they contact you?"

Priscilla sighed. "I'm trying hard to believe the best about you, Renee, but your hesitation to help when you know it's what Wanda wants makes it hard. She trusts you. How many others do?"

"It's none of your business."

"But if I have a reasonable concern that someone isn't dealing honestly, then I have to check it out. I truly hope it's only that we're not connecting."

"I don't appreciate the way you keep coming in here and accusing me of doing something wrong."

"I'm sorry it feels that way." Priscilla breathed a prayer for wisdom. "I just need to have better information. Are these even real names that you gave me?"

"What? Do you think I sit here all winter creating a list of names and numbers that no one will be able to trace or locate?"

Priscilla pulled out the list of names and placed it on the desk in front of Renee. "Then who are these people?"

Renee pointed to the top name, a Philip and Elaine Schnect. "This is a couple from New York. They come every year or two. They bounce around cottages but last year stayed in Wanda's." She slid her finger to the next entry. "And this woman brings her nieces with her. They make a week of it. I think they're from Rhode Island." Renee continued down the list with a story about each listing. "I don't know this name." She hesitated, then looked at the next to last name. "Or this one. That is unusual. I'm the one who checks people in and out most of the time. There were a couple of weekends I was gone last summer. They must have come during those times."

"You take off during the season?"

"You bet. I can only handle so many days when we're overrun by tourists before I need a quick break." Renee shrugged and glanced at her cell phone as it dinged. She picked up the device, read the screen, and the color drained from her face.

"Are you okay?"

"I'm f-fine." Her words stuttered, and she didn't seem to be listening.

"Renee, does this relate to the man at the garden center?"

"Why would you say that?"

"Because that's the only other time I've seen you this unsettled." Priscilla eased onto the edge of the chair in front of the desk. "Let me help you."

"Like you did at the Boardwalk? I think not." She pushed to her feet and shook her head as if clearing it. "I need to go." She had a frantic look in her eyes as she glanced around.

"Renee."

"There's an emergency with one of the cottages." Renee grabbed her purse and headed out the back.

Priscilla groaned and hurried after her. The woman had a lot to explain, and the more they talked, the longer the list of questions grew. Why was it so hard to be honest? What was Renee hiding?

When Priscilla stepped outside into the sunlight, it seemed as if Renee had vanished. Was it a trick of the sun? Priscilla squinted as she tried to spot her. A couple brushed past her, and she was pushed to the side. When she righted herself, she still couldn't find Renee.

Movement in the yard to the left caught her attention. The cottages were close enough together that there weren't traditional separated yards for most, and what existed in the back was as pocket-sized as the homes. She tracked the movement, but instead of spotting Renee, she spied a tall man striding along the back between houses. She squinted as she tried to see who it was.

"Renee, you can't run." His words were low and intense. "I will get what I came for. You know it, so go ahead and give it to me." He parted the branches of bushes as he passed as if he expected to find Renee hiding behind one.

As Priscilla reached for the phone in her purse and eased it free, the man noticed her.

"I wouldn't do that if I were you." He took a step toward her, then stopped as he watched her intently.

"What are you doing?" She was proud that her voice didn't tremble despite her internal quaking.

"I'm just trying to find a friend." He probably meant his smile to disarm her, but it was like the sneer of a hungry wolf.

"Is that why she's running from you?" She studied his face. Yep, it was the man from the garden center. His eyes didn't seem as soulless as the first time she'd seen him, but she still didn't want to be near him.

"You're making something out of nothing." He straightened the cuffs on his shirt. "Once Renee and I talk everything will be fine."

"Huh. Usually when someone is running from you, it means they aren't interested in talking."

"Or it could mean they don't understand what I'm looking for."

"Which is?"

"Something I entrusted to her care."

Priscilla studied him and tried not to grimace, because she could guess what that item was. She backed up a step. "Good luck with that."

He watched her but didn't say anything more. She turned and hurried away while trying not to make it obvious that she was scared. Once she crossed a yard, she turned to find him watching her. Then he took off in the direction he'd been going before he spotted her.

As soon as he walked away, Priscilla turned and returned to the office. She was hoping Renee had come back and would finally explain who that man was and what he wanted. But the office was empty, and there was no sign that Renee had returned at all.

Priscilla hurried across the grounds toward the parking lot where she'd left her car—and froze when she saw who was standing next to it.

CHAPTER TWENTY-THREE

What are you doing here?" This time she couldn't keep the tremble from her voice. The man had recognized her, or else he wouldn't have known which car was hers.

"All you have to do is tell me where it is." The man stepped closer.

"I don't know what you mean."

"I think you do." He took another step forward, and she stepped back.

"I don't know who you are or what you want, but this conversation is done." She turned to hurry away, her breathing hitched. A young man was passing a couple of rows up the lot, a travel bag hanging over his shoulder. He pulled a rolling suitcase behind him. "Sir." She held up her hand and waved. "Hey."

The man paused and turned to look around.

"Over here." Priscilla waved again.

The man who'd been intimidating her growled as he stepped away. "You'll regret this."

"I don't think so." Priscilla waved again, and the tourist finally spotted her.

He walked toward her. "Ma'am, is everything all right?"

"Is there any way you could escort me to my car?" Priscilla felt a trembling start in her fingers and creep over her body.

The young man hurried toward her as fast as his suitcase would allow. "Of course I can. Is there someone I can call for you?"

She fanned her face as she shook her head. "No, I'm headed straight to the police station." Officer Brown needed to know about this latest confrontation with the man from the garden center.

They reached her vehicle, and she held out her hand. "Thank you so much."

"No problem." The man stepped back. "I'll wait here until you're out of the lot."

The tension seeped from her shoulders as she considered him. "That would be a relief." She unlocked her door and slid in.

Her Good Samaritan kept his promise and waited as she backed out of the parking spot and then drove from the lot. It took her ten minutes to drive the three miles back to Vineyard Haven and the station, but it was only as she pulled into the station's parking lot that she felt the adrenaline finally leave her system. She hurried inside, and Gabrielle Grimes looked up from her desk with a frown. "You're here again?"

"This has been quite a week."

"I guess so. The chief told me about his trip out to your place last night." Gabrielle's expression softened. "Are you okay?"

"I am. Nothing was damaged, it's just unsettling."

"I imagine."

"Is Officer Brown in today?"

"She is, but I think she's at lunch. It's been busy, keeping the streets safe with the incoming tourists."

"Could you ask her if she has a minute? Please?"

The *please* seemed to make the difference, because Gabrielle sighed but reached for the phone and paged her. "Officer Brown, please come to the front. You have a guest." She hung up and turned back to Priscilla. "You can sit while we wait to see if she's coming."

"Thanks." Priscilla eased onto one of the old chairs and felt the tension return to her muscles. She rubbed her temples. The week was becoming too much, and she needed to release the stress. She closed her eyes and blew out a long breath as she asked God to help her put everything in His perspective. She took another deep breath that she released before she felt the knot inside begin to loosen.

It would be all right. Whether they ever discovered who owned the ship or not, all would be well.

The door separating the reception area from the rest of the police station opened, and April stepped through. She frowned at Gabrielle. "Who wants to see me?"

Gabrielle pointed to Priscilla. "Priscilla Grant is back."

Put that way, it sounded like she was a boomerang. She sighed and pushed to her feet. "Do you have a minute, Officer Brown?"

April considered her. "I'll make time." She held the door open for Priscilla. "What's going on? Well, other than someone breaking into your house."

"I had another odd interaction with the man from the garden center. Were you able to track down his name through his license plate?"

"Yes. I was going to call you and let you know. The man's name is Robert Gothard."

CHAPTER TWENTY-FOUR

B ob Gothard?" The man from the toy store? Priscilla pulled up her phone and tried to remember the name of the shop. Toy Menagerie? Was that it? She typed it into her search engine app and tapped her foot as she waited for the results to pop up.

"Does that name mean anything to you?"

"He's a toy appraiser Willow Gibson connected me with. We had a phone conversation on Tuesday and another one on Wednesday."

"Well, the car that was on the island is registered to him."

The search results finally appeared, and Priscilla frowned. The Robert Gothard pictured on the website looked a bit younger than the sixtyish man she'd seen on the island. Yet it was clearly the same person. "That's the man I've had confrontations with the last two days." She showed the picture to April.

"May I?" April took the phone from Priscilla and studied the image. "So he runs a toy store?"

"That's what Willow told me, and the website seems to back it up. He's supposedly something of an expert on toys, and Willow thought he might be able to help me by appraising our mystery ship." She glanced around, needing to sit. "This is getting more tangled all the time. Did he come to the island because of my call about the ship?"

April shrugged. "The only way to know is to ask him. Do you want to press charges against him? That would make it easier to bring him in."

Priscilla considered the question. Part of her did, but at the same time, she didn't know that he had done anything other than intimidate her and Renee. "I don't know."

"Well, think about it."

"Any thoughts on how to find Bob or Robert Gothard other than a warrant?"

"I can ask the other patrol officers to keep an eye out. But if you aren't willing to lodge a complaint, then there's not much we can do." April frowned. "Though it does sound like you're right, that he hasn't really done more than be intimidating—unless he's also the person who broke into your house."

"Sounds like I need to figure out why he wants that ship."

So many questions ran through her mind. Had the ship been stolen? Had Gothard been part of that, or had he seen the picture and knew the ship was valuable? Had he broken into her home?

She thanked April for her time. As she left the building her phone rang.

She was tempted to let it ring through to voice mail until she pulled it out of her pocket far enough to see it was her cousin. "Hi, Gail."

"Dad and Marigold would like to have the ceremony at two thirty Sunday afternoon followed by the reception at three. They hope to catch a ride to their honeymoon by five."

"Honeymoon? That's so sweet."

"It is, isn't it? The delivery company will bring everything out Saturday afternoon. Gives us a whole twenty-four hours to set up."

"It'll be perfect. I'm so glad I get to be part of this—although I won't be able to help you until Sunday morning. I'm helping Mildred all day Saturday with the show."

Gail snorted, then sighed, before she let out a nervous chuckle. "I'm a mess. I can't believe my dad is getting married, but at the same time, I'm relieved. She makes him so happy."

"And now your story can happen too."

"Well, I'm not counting on that. I've got a lot to wrap up. Thanks for everything."

"Sure."

"Oh, and don't forget the schools' Memorial Day celebrations tomorrow. We'll pick you up for the drive to Menemsha."

"Perfect. I'll see you then." Priscilla ended the call and climbed in her car. As she drove home, she couldn't stop her smile at the idea that her uncle was going to be married in three days on her property. It overshadowed every question she had about the ship and what had been happening.

Something beautiful was coming in the midst of the chaos.

CHAPTER TWENTY-FIVE

The sun danced in and out of the clouds as Priscilla and her cousins walked to the Menemsha Coast Guard station. Trudy was decked out in red capris with a blue and white striped shirt, while Joan wore a bedazzled red, white, and blue baseball cap. Gail wore a spangled flag shirt that left Priscilla feeling bland in her denim capris and red shirt. She slipped her sunglasses back on her nose as the sun came out again.

"It's going to be one of those days." Trudy grinned at them as she pulled out rhinestone-embellished sunglasses.

"All the tourists are begging for nonstop sunshine." Joan shook her head. "It's why I don't travel on holiday weekends. Invariably, the weather doesn't cooperate with everyone's plans."

Priscilla took in the small Coast Guard station. Twenty-four people worked at the station and maintained its grounds and two red-roofed white buildings. The main building was topped by a lighthouse-looking turret with a widow's walk. From a tall flag pole in front of it, the American flag flapped in the breeze, the Coast Guard flag flying directly beneath it.

Small American flags lined the path to the boathouse and pier that had been destroyed in a massive fire in 2010. The ribbon cutting on the new boathouse had only been three years earlier, and the construction crews had done a great job making the new structure look like it belonged at the station.

A small crowd had gathered in clusters on the grounds, and Buddy, the station's golden retriever mascot, was greeting people with dogged enthusiasm. His navy-blue collar was embroidered with his name and rank, something that would make Jake jealous if he were here. Good thing she'd left him back at the cottage. As she looked around, what seemed missing from the scene were the kids.

"Where are the children?" As Priscilla asked the question, school buses pulled into the parking area. "Never mind."

Trudy laughed. "You just need to be patient, Priscilla. When you're dealing with children, things don't go seamlessly."

Joan winked at Priscilla. "We've all had children, Trudy. We know the importance of being flexible when kids are involved."

Trudy shrugged. "Sometimes we need the reminder that life doesn't run on our schedule."

The children streamed from the buses and gathered on the green. Then a few adults handed out flowers to them. The kids were somber as they accepted the white and red carnations, as if they fully understood the significance of the day. Once every child had a flower, the teachers led them to the foot of the pier, the congregated adults watching with solemn expressions.

The children recited the Pledge of Allegiance, then a couple of them shared patriotic poems. One little boy, who must have been around eight, had an adorable lisp. A middle-school-aged girl stepped forward and led the crowd in singing "God Bless America."

As the last notes floated over the crowd, a recording of "Taps" started. The children turned and strolled to the end of the pier. There they released their flowers into the water.

Priscilla found it hard to release her breath as the children solemnly turned and strode single file back down the pier. "Wow. It looks like they found whoever they needed to organize the event. It was beautiful."

"It is impressive." Joan wiped her eyes surreptitiously.

The cousins waited for the students to pass, then turned toward Joan's vehicle. As they did, Priscilla stilled.

"What is it?" Gail looked around, trying to spot whatever Priscilla had seen.

"Is that Jerry Shire?"

Trudy frowned. "Who?"

"Jerry Shire. Wanda's son." Gail shook her head, then her eyes widened. "Wait, there he is. I thought he still lived off the island."

"He does," Priscilla said. "And he was pretty adamant that he wouldn't be back on the island for a while the last time I saw him."

"Well, he doesn't seem to want to be seen." Trudy pointed in the direction where he was slipping through a group of people his mother's age. "Do you think he brought Wanda out here?"

Gail scanned the group. "It doesn't look like it. I don't see a wheelchair in that mix."

"It would be tricky to navigate one across the ground here." Priscilla watched Jerry as he continued to push through the crowd. "Come on, gals. Let's see what he's doing here."

Joan put a hand on Priscilla's arm. "There's nothing wrong with him being here." She glanced around. "Look at everyone who came. All these events are published in our newspaper, so it's not a surprise that the events are happening. In fact, they're tradition on the island."

"You're right. This ship has me in knots." Priscilla forced a smile as she turned from watching Jerry. "Let's head on out."

"Without saying hello?" The familiar deep voice stopped Priscilla in her tracks.

"We'll see you at the car." Trudy had the audacity to wink at her, and the cousins continued on their way.

"I always knew I liked her." Gerald's voice was warm and his hands warmer as he put them on her shoulders. "Fancy seeing you here."

"The girls talked me into checking out the festivities."

"It's a little solemn to be called festive, but the students enjoy it." Gerald looked over the crowd with a practiced eye. "Turnout is good this year. The cooler temperatures probably helped attendance."

Priscilla nodded as she felt the whisper of the breeze. "I can understand why people come out for it. The poems were nice."

"And that young lady can sing."

"She can." Priscilla took a step back, and Buddy trotted up. "So how's this guy?"

"Enjoying being our mascot." Gerald stooped down and rubbed the dog's ears. "Aren't you, boy?"

"He seems to really enjoy the crowd."

"He's great with people. Better than some of my Coasties." Gerald chuckled.

"I love that." Priscilla glanced toward Joan's vehicle and spied her cousins leaning against it. "I'd better catch up with them."

"Can I pick you up tomorrow to go to the museum?"

"That would be great. About nine-thirty should be good." She felt the warmth of his farewell embrace as she walked to the car.

"Let's go," Joan said. "If we want to get to town for the March to the Sea, we need to move."

Gail glanced at her watch then at her cousin. "But it's only ten-thirty."

"You know we need a good spot. And a stop at Candy's. I didn't get my coffee this morning."

"Since you're driving, I think you get to dictate where we go." Trudy slipped into the back seat. "Besides, I'm always ready for one of Candy's scones. It's keeping it off my hips that's challenging."

Priscilla listened to the back-and-forth with contentment. She climbed in the passenger side of the SUV and sank back against the seat. The Menemsha station was on the far side of the island, a twenty-five-minute drive from Vineyard Haven. As they drove, they passed the Martha's Vineyard Glassworks. She hadn't been there since September but was eager to explore it again when she had more time.

In a few more minutes, Joan was driving them into Vineyard Haven and finding a parking spot in front of Candy's. When they entered it looked like a book club of about ten had collected several tables and chairs and was engaged in discussion. The women were leaning in, and one was waving her arms in such a way that a mug could go flying.

Candy swept around the corner, a harried look on her face. "Hello, ladies. What can I get you today?"

Trudy wanted a scone and coffee, and Joan ordered her traditional cream puff and coffee. "I'll also take an orange-cranberry muffin to go." When Trudy's mouth opened, Joan shrugged it off. "What? I want to get tomorrow's breakfast now."

"I wish I could do that." Trudy took the plated scone from Candy and sighed dramatically.

"So what's your diet of the month, Trudy?" Gail teased. "If you'd just pick one diet and stick to it, you wouldn't have to worry."

"Maybe. I know there are probably better choices I could make here, but I don't care. Candy makes the best scones." She lifted the plate as if it was exhibit A. "I have a love-hate relationship with food. Love it too much, and then it hates me."

Candy laughed as she slid a muffin in a bag for Joan. "I'll take that as a compliment."

"You should." Trudy sailed to a table.

Priscilla stepped to the counter. "I'll take an orange-cranberry muffin and coffee."

Candy glanced at Gail.

"I'll just have a tea." As her cousins stared at her, she stared back. "What? I already had two cups of coffee this morning. If I have any more, I'll get jittery, and nobody wants that. It's not pretty."

Candy filled a mug with coffee for Priscilla then another with hot water for Gail. "The teabags are on the counter."

"Thanks."

As Gail doctored her tea, Priscilla paid for their snacks. Once the four were seated at a table, the conversation turned to Uncle Hugh and Marigold.

Gail stirred her tea long enough to make butter if it had been milk. "I'll be glad when it's behind us. For a couple who just wants to get married, they're making it harder than they need to."

"What do you mean?" Joan leaned into the table, both hands around her mug.

"They keep inviting people and then feel hurt when the notice is too short for many of them to come."

Priscilla frowned. "That's part of choosing a holiday weekend on short notice when so many people travel."

"You and I know that, but I'm afraid they're going to be disappointed. On a positive note, I've ordered a batch of cupcakes from Candy."

"I'll have them ready Saturday evening." Candy walked by with the coffeepot.

"And they'll taste great. It's the rest that I'm worried about."

Priscilla put her hand over Gail's. "I got the yard mowed yesterday and planted some roses and perennials. So the backdrop will be nice. All that matters is that they get to spend their future together. The wedding is just one day."

Gail nodded, but she didn't look convinced. "I just want them pleased at the end."

"Don't take on too much burden." Trudy took a bite of her scone. "Women do that all the time, and it drives us crazy. Focus on them and not on what might go wrong."

"Besides, you know we'll all show up to help. Just tell us when and where."

Gail smiled at them, and it reached her eyes for the first time since they'd sat at the table. "I love you three."

Priscilla leaned over and gave her a one-armed hug. "We love you right back."

By the time the cousins finished their treats and conversation, Joan was trying to hurry them along. "The students will leave the school any minute."

Trudy slowed down. "We don't need to follow them from Tisbury School all the way to the dock. Let's pick them up along Main Street."

Gail nodded. "That would keep us out of their way."

Joan looked at Priscilla. "Have an opinion?"

"Oh, no. Remember this is my first time watching all the festivities. We'll see the entire parade no matter where we stand on the route."

It was a short walk from Candy's Beach Road location to Main Street. Priscilla glanced around the crowd. A few faces looked familiar, like they might have been at the Coast Guard station a couple of hours earlier and were now ready to participate in another school's Memorial Day observances.

Then she turned and saw Jerry again. Was he following her, or were his appearances simply coincidental? She didn't want to be paranoid, but since someone had broken into her house, she felt cautious. Uncertain in ways she hadn't before.

"You okay?" Gail's question startled Priscilla.

"Yeah. I'm fine." The parade began to pass by, and Priscilla focused on the students, who were a mix of somber and excited. A few seemed to think they were on display and were enjoying every moment. Next to them, others were focused on the road, as if they'd rather be anywhere else. It happened at every event involving children. Those who loved the spotlight and those who wanted to disappear. Rachel had always been comfortable on stage without the need to be the center of attention. It had made every Christmas and school program less stressful for all of them.

As the last child passed by, the crowd watching on the sidewalk folded in and followed them up Main Street, then turned into Owen Park and proceeded to the dock. A high school band waited there and played some rousing Sousa marches. A group of children walked around handing out flags to the watchers. Soon the area around the dock was awash with waving flags, the somber mood abandoned to enjoy the music and the holiday.

Priscilla saw Jerry again, but this time Renee was standing next to him. She was speaking to him, and if her face and body language were any indication, it was a serious issue. Priscilla leaned over to whisper to Gail. "I'm going to slide that way."

Gail followed her eyes and nodded. "Be careful."

"Always." She wanted to get to the bottom of what had brought Jerry back to the island and why he was chatting with Renee. She took a deep breath as she stepped between several people in the crowd. *Lord, help me to see only what's really there. I don't want to be suspicious if it's nothing.*

What she wanted was answers for Wanda and for herself. After all the time she'd spent searching, she was vested in the outcome. Maybe even more than Wanda was.

She needed answers because *American Antiques* would be examining items the next day. Right now, she still wasn't sure if showing the ship was the best course of action. Was it even Wanda's to show? Under a finders-keepers approach, yes. Maybe she just needed to relax into that.

And maybe she needed to keep asking questions until she figured out how Jerry, Renee, and Bob Gothard were all connected.

As she got within ten feet of Jerry and Renee, they still hadn't noticed her, and their conversation wasn't exactly quiet or subtle.

"I need that ship now." Renee's words were frantic. The breeze tugged at the brim of her hat, which revealed a face as tense as her voice.

"I don't have it, and you know that." Jerry shoved his hands in his pockets. "It's not my fault that you didn't get it when you had the chance."

"You could have warned me your mom was having someone else open the cottage. By the time I got in there, the only thing I got were those worthless wooden toys."

Jerry snorted. "That would require her to tell me." He stepped closer to Renee. "This has gotten bigger than you said it would."

"Some things are out of my control, Jerry." Renee took a step back from Jerry then another before running out of room.

Priscilla slipped behind a large man to try and stay out of their line of sight.

"When you got me to help, you made promises. I expect those to be kept." Jerry's smile wasn't friendly. "You don't want me to ask for an accounting of your use of the cabin."

Renee turned and stared at him. "You wouldn't do that."

"I might. Mom's friend is asking some interesting questions that have me thinking about the money I'm not seeing." He stood practically toe to toe with her now. "The agreement was you use the cottage, and I get half the money." He rubbed his thumb against his index and middle fingers. "So where is it?"

"Be quiet." Her gaze flitted around, and then she stiffened. Had she seen Priscilla?

Priscilla decided she might as well approach them. She made a show of startling when she saw Jerry. "I didn't expect to see you here. What brings you back?"

"I guess you could call it nostalgia. Mom used to drag us to these events. I may have even walked in a few of these parades." His lip slipped up in the corner as if he remembered something good. Renee took a step back and then another, but he stopped her with a hand on her arm. She tried to slip free, but he held on. "If you'll excuse us, Priscilla, we have some things we need to discuss."

"Of course." Her mind was spinning after what she'd over-heard. Or would they expect her to be nosy? She took a breath and dived in. "Will you be here for the *American Antiques* filming tomorrow? I bet your mom would love the escort."

"I don't know." Jerry shrugged. "It depends on what happens tonight."

"Oh?"

"If I get a call that my sons need me, I'll be back on the mainland in short order."

"Ah. I see." She smiled. "Well, enjoy the rest of the day." She turned back toward the parade route, but sensed when the two slipped away. She shifted to watch them and noted that they made no pretense of heading in different directions.

Why would they be working together and using the cottage in off-the-record ways? Wanda hadn't given any indication she was aware of the use other than letting Adam Reeling use it. If Jerry and Renee worked together to rent the cottage during the off-season, that could be a lot of money to split. And if Renee was doing that with other cottages, she could be pocketing quite a sum over the time the campgrounds were largely abandoned in the winter. Since there was so little parking around the cottages, the traffic in and out of the property might not be noticed. Especially if it was just a few vehicles here or there.

That still didn't explain the ship.

Priscilla tried to focus on the kids walking by, but her thoughts spun. Renee needed the ship, but Jerry was blaming her for not getting it in time. Could they be desperate enough to break into her house? It was possible.

Priscilla walked back to where her cousins watched the elementary kids march by.

"Any luck?" Joan asked.

"I overheard something, but I'm not sure what to do with it."

"Can we help?" Gail seemed uncertain about whether to ask or wait.

Priscilla shrugged. "Let's enjoy the rest of the ceremony, and then we can talk."

The last child walked by. Everyone walked across Owen Park, to the pier, where the children one by one solemnly threw their flowers into the water.

There was something touching about the simplicity of the action and the way the flower drop was repeated over and over. One child would step forward, to be followed by another. Again and again, until each child had taken part. Then they turned and started back across the park. As soon as the last student passed by again, Trudy headed toward a picnic table.

"All right. Time to tell us what's going on." She patted the bench she was sitting on. "Spill the beans, Priscilla."

Gail slipped beneath the table on the other side. "I need to hear what's got you bothered."

Priscilla sighed. "That's just it. I'm not sure if I'm onto something, or just seeing things that aren't really there." But the conversation she'd overheard was pretty plain. "Renee and Jerry were arguing about a ship that Renee needed to get back. Jerry said it was her fault she hadn't retrieved it when she had a chance." She

208 | MYSTERIES of MARTHA'S VINEYARD

turned to Gail. "They had to be talking about us finding the ship at Wanda's cottage."

"How did he think she should have gotten it first? Gone into the cabin before we did?"

"I think so. What if they broke into my house?" She shook her head. "Jerry couldn't have, because he was at Wanda's. But he could have let Renee know I wasn't home. And then worked to keep me there."

Joan eased onto the bench, next to Gail. "That's a serious allegation, Priscilla."

"I know." She rubbed her shoulder. "What am I supposed to do with this?"

"Maybe mention it to Officer Brown." Gail shrugged. "Did she ever get back to you about thefts?"

"Just what the chief told me. That it was too early to know if things had disappeared from the cottages over the winter."

Trudy tapped the tabletop with her fingers. "We can stop at the police station on our way out of town."

"No, they're too busy. And I was there yesterday. They'll think I'm creating excuses to visit."

"Well, we're running out of time." Gail pushed from the table. "Wanda is determined to take the ship to the taping tomorrow and see what Tim and Cherish can tell her." She met Priscilla's gaze. "She really wants to meet them and says the ship is her best opportunity. She may not have expected that to be in her cottage, but she's glad it was."

Priscilla smiled at the image of Wanda telling Gail that she would take the ship to the museum to use it as her ticket to meet celebrities. "It will be interesting to hear what they say about it."

"True." Joan glanced at her watch and then pushed to her feet and joined Gail next to the table. "Let's grab a bite for lunch, and then we can get to work on the reception food."

Priscilla's phone rang, showing a familiar number on the display, and she picked up the call. "Hi, Mildred."

"I need help, now." The panicked tone in Mildred's voice had Priscilla meeting Joan's gaze. "The TV crew is here."

CHAPTER TWENTY-SIX

Mildred rushed out of the museum and down the steps before Priscilla could climb out of Joan's car.

"Thank goodness you're here."

"What's going on?"

Mildred had a slightly wild look in her eyes as she tugged Priscilla up the steps. "The film crew got here two hours ago. Since then they've broken an antique picture frame and muddied one of the carpets."

Priscilla glanced around. "It hasn't rained in a couple of days."

"I know, but somehow they managed to find the only mud on the island." Mildred deflated. "What am I supposed to do about them when they won't listen to me?"

"They work for an antiques show. I'm sure we can get them to be more careful when we explain why it's necessary. They knew this was a museum, right?"

Mildred's eyebrows arched, and her skepticism was clear. "Wait until you meet them."

"Are Tim and Cherish here?"

"Not yet. Frankly, I'm not sure that would improve anything." Mildred opened the front door, and Priscilla froze.

One technician was taping strands of cords to the floor, his strong hands ripping the duct tape, the sound echoing in the hall entry, making it seem smaller than normal. Another technician hurried from the kitchen, her ponytail swinging behind her as she carried a roll of paper towels.

"Oh no." Mildred groaned. "What did they break or spill now?"

"Take a deep breath. We don't know anything yet." Priscilla steered her friend to follow the young woman into the dining room where a pool of syrupy-looking liquid spread across an antique table from an overturned paper cup.

Mildred straightened, and her shoulders thrust back as she strode toward the woman. "All right. That is enough. You are all done in here until you can prove to me you'll handle the museum's collection with dignity and care."

"I am so sorry, Mrs. Pearson. I didn't realize John had left his drink here."

"Anna, I'm not sure how you could miss it." Mildred sputtered the words. "It's practically the size of a bucket."

"I'll get it all cleaned up and make sure we take our drinks outside." Anna looked sufficiently chastised. "This isn't how we normally operate, but we're several hours behind schedule. That doesn't mean we should be careless though, and I'm sincerely sorry about that." She had mopped up the mess as she talked, and Mildred's shoulders slowly relaxed.

Mildred sighed. "Everything in here has been carefully collected and displayed."

"I understand, ma'am." The young woman sighed again. "I am so sorry. Can we keep working if we promise to be careful?"

"As long as I have someone's credit card."

Anna's eyes bugged. "Ma'am?"

"If anything else gets broken, I want to know who's paying for it."

Anna went to the doorway. "Joe?"

The man looked up from where he was taping. "Yeah?"

"I need your credit card."

"Why's that?"

"Because it's the best way to make sure you're careful."

Joe grumbled, but he reached in his back pocket, tugged out his wallet, and pulled a credit card out of it. "How about we leave it here on this table?"

"Oh, no." Anna grabbed the card and handed it to Mildred. "Here you go. Now can we continue?"

Mildred nodded as she slipped the card in her apron pocket. "Please understand, I don't want to use this, but I will. You must be careful, because I can't walk into some home-décor store and replace these items. These are treasures."

"Understood." Joe lowered his head and sounded contrite as he went back to work.

"When will Tim and Cherish arrive?" Mildred directed the question to Anna.

"Whenever they get off the ferry." Her attention diverted back to the dining room. "I have to finish getting the dining room set up, then we'll head upstairs."

"Let's get out of her way and get something to drink." Priscilla led Mildred to the kitchen. There she pulled two bottles of water from the fridge and saw trays of fruit and vegetables stacked and ready to go. A tray of sweets sat next to the refrigerator. "Looks like you're ready for tomorrow."

"If food is all it takes, we're golden." Mildred leaned against the sink and sighed. "This feels big."

"You should have a few extra people checking out the museum. *American Antiques* has quite a following."

"Yes, but I'm not sure it's worth it." Mildred accepted a water bottle from Priscilla and sighed again as she twisted the cap off. "I'm not sure I would have said yes if I'd known what was going to happen."

"Of course you would have. You love a challenge and showing off what you've accomplished here."

"But that's it. I'm not sure this does. With all the extra equipment and lighting, no one will see the simplicity of what we've accomplished." Mildred took a drink of her water as she glanced around the kitchen. "I have visions of making this historically accurate as well. Just haven't done it yet."

"Yes you have. It's just reflective of the 1990s." Priscilla laughed as Mildred sputtered. "There's a generation who doesn't know what that looks like. But they should."

"Now you're just making fun."

"No, I'm trying to help you relax into the adventure. People are going to love your museum."

Mildred sighed as she set her water on the counter. "This just isn't how I imagined it."

"That's because it's more chaotic than you expected. It'll settle down."

"I don't think so. Did you know Joyce Roberts has insisted she wants to bring a suit of armor? How does she think she's going to transport it?"

Priscilla laughed at the bewilderment on Mildred's face. "I think that's her problem if she chooses to bring it. She can always have it evaluated from the porch."

"The lighting would be terrible." Joe's voice reached them, and Priscilla covered her mouth to stifle a laugh.

"Guess we should talk somewhere else so we don't bother them."

"You're not bothering us." This time it was Anna's voice. Then she stepped into view. "Is it okay if I head upstairs?"

Mildred hesitated. "Can you explain again what you want to do?"

"Maybe it would be better if I showed you." Anna waited for Mildred to nod, then turned to Priscilla. "Sorry I didn't introduce myself earlier. I'm Anna Wilcox, production technician for the show."

"Priscilla Grant, Mildred's friend."

"And sanity." Mildred spoke the words from the side of her mouth.

Anna must have heard. "Then I'm glad you're here. Will you be back tomorrow?"

"Yes. I'm curious to see the process from behind the camera."

"Let's say it's loosely organized chaos. Mildred wasn't too far off." Anna's smile brightened her face. "Can we go on up?"

Mildred nodded. "I'd like to hear what you want to do."

Anna spent the next ten minutes demonstrating how she expected to use the space upstairs. "We can have people set up on these tables. It will give them the best chance to display their items...well, except for that armor." She glanced at Mildred. "Do you think she'll really bring that?"

"No idea. Joyce is the kind of person who will get a crazy idea in her head and keep chasing it."

"Sounds fun and interesting." Anna glanced around. "If she decides to bring it, I'm sure we'll find a way to showcase it. That's what Tim and Cherish are so good at. Do you understand what we want to do and why?"

"I think so." Mildred glanced around with a worried wrinkle between her eyes. "This area is where we store our documents, and the contents of the files are actually more important than most of what is downstairs."

The cabinets in the large room housed journals and newspapers, as Priscilla had learned in the hours she'd spent in that research space. It could feel spartan, but it was organized well for its purpose, and the items were irreplaceable.

Mildred looked around with pride in her eyes. "You should have seen it before I was hired. It was a true hodgepodge and almost impossible to find anything. It took a while, but I'm pleased with how it's turned out. It's a workable area for genealogical research,

and many researchers come to the island for the purpose of searching these records."

"You must be very proud of it." There was a buzz, and Anna
looked down at the phone clipped to her belt. "Excuse me."

Priscilla watched her head back downstairs, then turned to
Mildred. "I don't understand why you were concerned. She seems
delightful."

"Sure, but you weren't here before I got the credit card.
Hopefully I won't need to use it." Mildred patted her apron pocket
as if confirming it was still there. "I'm not sure I'm ready for
tomorrow."

"It'll be fine. I can plan to be here most of the day to help."

"I'll take you up on that offer. I thought I could handle this on
my own, but now I see how easily it could spiral out of control."
Mildred looked from side to side. "I can't have people digging
through the files. Can you imagine what could happen if kids got
into them?" She sighed.

"Nothing that couldn't be reorganized."

"As long as they don't tear up a journal or shred the last copy
of a newspaper."

Priscilla had to smile at the hyperbole. "Last time I checked,
kids don't usually walk around looking for things to shred."

"I'm stressing out over what-ifs that will probably never happen." Mildred rolled her eyes. "I know you're right. Besides if anything happens, I have that young man's credit card."

"That you do." Priscilla glanced around the room. "Let's move
the tables so they're in front of the file cabinets, and people have to

walk in the middle of the room. That should minimize people getting into places they aren't supposed to be."

The two women set to work shifting the heavy library-style tables. The surfaces would give those bringing items to be evaluated a good place to set their treasures without distraction. Priscilla couldn't imagine too many people bringing their young children with them—the event would be no fun for them—but now there were barriers in place to help keep them out of trouble.

As they finished, Anna and Joe made their way upstairs, lugging gear.

"Be careful," Mildred called out, but not before Joe banged into the wall. "Son, you have got to be careful."

"I hear you."

Priscilla was surprised Mildred didn't let him know what she thought of his attitude.

A clamor on the first floor drew Mildred to the top of the stairs. Before she descended, she looked over her shoulder. "Don't destroy anything while I'm downstairs, okay?"

Priscilla tapped Anna's shoulder. "We tried to arrange the tables to block the files but also provide the best way to move around. Let us know if you need them somewhere else."

"Oh, Joe can help me move them if necessary."

"Great. Then I'm going to see where else Mildred needs help."

Anna and Joe were unzipping their bags before Priscilla had left the newly open reading space. As they pulled out extension cords and other technical gear, Priscilla was glad to leave them to it and head back to things she understood. It would be fascinating to watch them in action in the morning, but for now she felt the need to stick close to Mildred. Her friend was absorbing a large amount of stress about the event.

Priscilla stilled as she reached the bottom of the stairs. A man and a woman stood near the desk talking with Mildred. Priscilla swallowed against a suddenly dry throat. Tim and Cherish had arrived.

CHAPTER TWENTY-SEVEN

The hosts of *American Antiques* had stopped to shake hands with Mildred.

Cherish looked around the museum's first-floor rooms. "This space is as charming as I remembered." She slowly turned. "It looks like Joe and Anna have been hard at work."

Mildred tilted her head to one side in a partial shrug. "Anna, yes, Joe, meh."

Tim laughed at the characterization. "Sounds about right. I bet Anna's been keeping Joe in line."

Priscilla stepped onto the first floor, and Mildred motioned her forward. "I'd like you to meet my friend Priscilla Grant. You'll likely see her around here tomorrow. If you need anything and can't find me, Priscilla is your gal."

"Well, then, it's nice to meet you." Tim reached forward and shook her hand. Hers felt small in his large one. Everything about the man seemed oversized. He was tall, sturdy, and broad in the shoulders, but his jeans and polo shirt with the show's logo on it made him seem approachable.

Cherish watched Priscilla.

Tim nudged her. "Aren't you going to say hi?"

Cherish startled and smiled. "Of course. You caught me in la-la land, I guess. It's a pleasure to meet you."

"And you. I've really enjoyed the episodes of *American Antiques* that I've caught." Priscilla cringed a bit. "I don't get much time to watch TV, but if I had more I'm sure I'd watch more of your show." She glanced at Mildred, feeling a rising panic at the inane things spilling from her mouth. "I'm usually not so clumsy with words."

"Happens to the best of us." Tim grinned at her, and a dimple appeared in the center of his chin.

As Priscilla felt Tim's charm weave around her, she decided Wanda had to come meet the two hosts. She was so enthusiastic about the show that Priscilla could imagine how she'd moon over a grin like the one Tim had flashed in her direction.

An hour later when Mildred drove Priscilla home, she texted Gail. *Just met Tim and Cherish. We have to bring Wanda to the show tomorrow. She'll swoon.*

A minute later her cousin responded. *Already have that planned. Want to ride with us?*

Gerald and I will meet you there. About 9:45?

They finished arranging the details as Mildred pulled into Priscilla's driveway. "You promise you'll be there tomorrow to help?"

"As much or as little as you need. Gerald is going to pick me up at nine thirty, and I'll plan to stay and help you even if he has to leave."

"How will you get home?"

"Either the same way I did now, or I'll get a cab."

"I can give you a ride. So long as I don't have to stay at the museum all night while they undo all their gear."

"You won't, and if you do, I'll stay with you."

"Thank you."

Mildred pulled out as Priscilla entered her house. As she walked by the living room, she paused and looked at the ship.

"Tomorrow we're going to find out what you're worth."

Jake looked at her with curious eyes, and she absently rubbed his ears. Maybe Tim and Cherish could tell her something that would explain why Jerry, Renee, and Bob Gothard were all tied up with this ship.

Saturday morning Priscilla dressed with care. While she didn't plan to get anywhere near a camera, she wanted to be prepared. Gerald pulled into the driveway precisely at nine thirty, and he carefully carried the ship to his car. When she reached the car, she smiled because Wanda sat stretched out in the back, her leg propped on the seat.

"I thought Gail was going to collect Wanda." Then Priscilla glanced through the car's very back window and saw Gail.

Priscilla got in the passenger seat, and Gerald handed her the ship. "Gail called me this morning and asked if she and Wanda could ride with us because her car wouldn't start. Jerry helped us get Wanda into the car."

"Jerry was there?"

"Oh yes," Wanda chimed in. "That son of mine decided to spend the night. I never know what he's going to do." She shrugged. She wore a royal-purple sweater paired with white capris and bedazzled sandals. Her white hair was coiffed in perfect curls that looked like she'd just stepped out of the stylist's chair. A bangled necklace in purple and red and a matching bracelet tied the look together. Wanda looked excited to have her fifteen minutes of fame. "I see you have my ship."

"I do." Priscilla turned and looked at her. "Decided it's yours?"

"No one has claimed it, and it was found in my cottage." The woman shrugged her thin shoulders. "That makes it mine."

Priscilla couldn't argue with her logic as she met Gail's gaze in the rearview mirror. Her cousin smiled as Gerald started the car and backed down the driveway.

"Come on, kiddo. Pedal to the metal so we aren't late." Wanda's words were snappy and spirited.

Priscilla laughed as Gerald made a show of pressing down on the gas pedal. "The program orientation doesn't start until ten, Wanda," she said. "Gerald will get us there in plenty of time."

"That's what they all say." Wanda harrumphed good-naturedly. "I don't have many years left. Can't waste them wondering about what-ifs."

"You hardly seem like you have one foot in the grave." Priscilla couldn't think of another woman with as much spunk. "Just look at how well you're bouncing back from your surgery."

"That was peanuts. A mere trifle now that my moment of fame beckons." Wanda fluffed her curls as Gerald turned into town.

The drive to the East Shore Historical Museum had flown by, thanks to Wanda's banter. Cars filled the parking lot, and people were congregated on the front porch.

"Why don't you ladies wait in the car while I slip inside and see if they're ready for us." Gerald put the car in Park and unbuckled his seat belt.

"We can delay my arrival." Wanda placed one hand in her lap regally, then waved the other in a gentle side to side motion that looked exactly like something the British royals would do.

Priscilla rolled her eyes and nodded at Gerald. "I'll come with you."

She climbed out and settled the ship on the seat, then hustled up the stairs with Gerald. They wove around the line to work their way through the front door. She heard some murmuring behind her but didn't slow. When the door closed behind them, she paused to identify where the show's hosts were. Mildred stood to one side watching as Tim and Cherish took another look around the museum that was moonlighting as a set.

"Didn't I tell you this would be perfect?" Cherish grinned at Tim. She wore a simple teal blouse over designer jeans with cowboy boots peeking out the bottom. Her hair was styled and her makeup applied to perfection. Up close, Priscilla could see how caked on it was. Must be a necessity of the lights and cameras, because she'd had a wholesome, natural look the prior day, and looked beautiful.

"I agree it will work well. Nice find." Tim had planted his fists on his hips and was surveying the space. "We'll have to regulate how many are inside at a time." Tim wore a gray button-down paired with dark jeans and porter boots. His dark hair was slicked to the side on the top and short on the sides, and with his glasses gave off a hipster vibe.

They turned when they spotted her.

Cherish smiled and took a step forward. "You're back."

There was something slightly familiar about her voice, but that was probably because Priscilla had watched the show. "I am." She introduced Gerald to the couple. "Do you need anything before you get started?"

Her words seemed to startle Mildred out of whatever fog had enveloped her. "Yes. What can I help with? There are a lot of people gathered on the porch already."

"We'll be sending our people out in a few minutes to organize them. We'd initially thought to have them all wait upstairs and bring them down, but that really doesn't flow well with this layout. Looks like Anna was right again. There's too much chance something will be harmed." Cherish nibbled her lower lip as she considered the space. "Since the weather is nice, let's have them wait on the porch and then bring them inside. If the porch gets overwhelmed, we can take them upstairs in groups of five or ten."

Mildred nodded. "That should work. Who do you want to start with?"

"You can pick the first one."

Priscilla glanced at Mildred. "How about Wanda Shire? I don't want her out there longer than necessary. She's still recovering from her surgery. Her wheelchair will take up a lot of space too."

"That should work." Mildred moved toward the front door. "Why don't you all get her, and I'll get the others organized."

"Sounds like a plan." Priscilla followed Gerald outside and walked toward the car. But when she saw it, the passenger door was open, and Gail was standing outside the car on her phone. Priscilla heard pounding feet and glanced in that direction. Two young men sprinted down the sidewalk at speeds she could never hope to match. What on earth? She hurried to Wanda's door. "What's going on?"

"A young woman came and opened the car door and grabbed the ship."

Priscilla deflated. "Was it Renee?"

"I...I can't be sure. She was wearing a hoodie with the hood pulled over her face. Those two young men took off after her." Wanda wrung her hands. "Do you think they'll catch her?"

Priscilla looked at the two men running down the street. "Yes, they seem very fast."

Gail hung up and turned to Gerald. "Officer Brown is on her way. Can you believe the brazenness? We were sitting in the car, and that woman opened the door and snagged the ship. In front of all these people. Doesn't she understand someone will recognize her? And it's so large and heavy, there's no way she can get away."

"Maybe she has someone ready to take it from her." Because Gail was right. Renee or whoever was running with the ship, must not have realized how heavy and awkward it was. She wouldn't get far without being caught. Priscilla turned her attention to Wanda, who was reclining on the back seat. "Wanda, they wanted you to go first."

"Oh, really?" She smiled and began to shift in the car. "Then let's get ready. Someone needs to get my wheelchair out of the back. I don't get fifteen minutes of fame every day, you know."

Priscilla hated to pop her enthusiasm. "Without the ship, they don't have anything to look at."

"That's all right. One of those guys was our track star last year. If anyone can bring the ship back, Aidan can."

And Wanda was right. Five minutes later, as a police vehicle pulled up, the two young men were walking back, one holding the ship and the other bringing the woman. Her hood had slid back, revealing her face.

Renee.

CHAPTER TWENTY-EIGHT

Priscilla sighed as she watched Renee approach with an expression of defiance and defeat. When Renee spotted the police car, her face drained of color, and she tried to pull free from the grip of the young man.

"Please, you have to let me go." Her words were edged with panic. "Just take the ship."

"Why did you take it?" Priscilla stepped up to Renee and repeated the question when Renee ducked her head. "Is it a valuable antique?"

"You don't want to know."

"Actually, after all the time I've spent on this ship the last week, you owe me an answer. Especially if you've known all along." Priscilla sighed. "You sent me on enough goose chases to frustrate even the most peaceful of people."

"I'm sorry, but I had to get it back before someone figured out where it came from."

"If this all was really so dangerous, why didn't you just call the police?" Gail asked.

"Bob threatened me. I didn't think I had any other choice." Renee's voice shook as she spoke.

Officer April Brown stepped into the group, interrupting her tête-à-tête with Gerald. "I think you need to back this conversation up, and start at the beginning. What's going on?"

Gail met the officer's gaze. "This woman reached into the car and stole that ship." She jerked her chin toward the ship.

April nodded toward her squad car. "Miss, I'd like you to have a seat in my car while I figure out what happened." She turned toward Priscilla. "Did you see any of this?"

"No, I was inside." Priscilla scanned the porch. "Wanda was going to be first on the show, so I was coming outside to get her, but when I got out here, the passenger door was open, the young men were running after Renee, and the ship was gone."

A woman called down from the porch. "She walked up cool as a cucumber, opened the door, and bolted with the ship in her hands."

"Is the woman in my car the one you saw take the ship?"

"Yes, ma'am."

April looked at the ship. "That doesn't seem worth stealing."

"I wouldn't think so either," Priscilla agreed.

"Brings us back to your idea that thieves might be using the cottages to hide goods."

"Yes." Priscilla turned over the idea that Renee might know how to open the ship.

"You have a theory?" Officer Brown's words weren't really a question.

"I think so, but it's not quite falling together."

"You have no idea what you're involved in." Dread filled Renee's voice. "Please let me go."

"Ma'am. That's not possible until I have a better idea what happened." April turned back to Priscilla. "Just to confirm, is this the ship you asked me about earlier in the week?"

"Yes."

"And no one has stepped forward to claim it?"

"No."

"And you found it in Wanda Shire's cottage, right?"

"Yes."

Wanda leaned out of the car window. "Can I take it inside to see what Tim and Cherish think about it?"

"Maybe. Let me call the chief. I'd have to stay with you for chain of custody purposes. And that means someone else will have to come collect Miss Overman." She stepped away and a minute later returned. "The chief will come get her. I'll interview witnesses and collect their information and then we can take you inside, Wanda. Gerald, will you stay with Miss Overman?" Gerald nodded and went to stand by the squad car.

"That's fine." Wanda reached across the car and patted Gail's hand. "Gail is taking good care of me."

Priscilla slipped next to the young men and asked them to stay near the car and ship while she went inside to update Mildred. She found her friend hiding in the kitchen. "What are you doing in here?"

"Getting away from the chaos." Mildred shuddered. "It's as overwhelming as I feared. People have forgotten this is a museum, not a zoo."

"Well, for one day, it'll be more the latter. But it will be over and back to normal soon." Priscilla glanced around. Tim was in the dining room examining a painting, and Cherish stood in the parlor, studying an odd-looking little statue. It amazed her that they knew enough to find the unique features in such divergent items. She couldn't wait to learn what they made of the ship. She just hoped it was enough to satisfy Wanda and her thirst for a moment in the spotlight.

"So what happened out there?"

"A woman stole Wanda's ship, but we have it back. Officer Brown is going to stay with her so Tim or Cherish can look at it. Do you think they'll know what it is?"

Mildred shrugged, then smiled. "If anyone will, they will. It's impressive to watch them shift from object to object. Tim over there just valued an old family journal. It's quite the process. They can really think on their feet."

"We're waiting on Chief Westin to come collect Renee Overman and Officer Brown to conduct witness interviews. It's a little unusual to let someone hang on to what might be evidence, but I'm glad they're making a way." She smiled at the way her small island came together for its people. "It will mean so much to Wanda. Let me go see if Officer Brown is ready."

"Cherish said she'd stop after whichever person she was with as soon as Wanda's ready."

"That's great." The host was really impressing Priscilla with her down-to-earth approach. "I'll be back with Wanda as fast as I can."

"And I'll go monitor my museum." Mildred pushed away from the kitchen counter. "Back into the fray."

When Priscilla got outside, Gerald came to her side. More people had joined the line, but they all seemed to be having a good time as they talked about their items with each other. April saw Priscilla and walked toward her.

"I've gotten what I need, and Chief Westin has come and gone with Renee. Let's get Wanda inside, and then I'll take the ship with me back to the station." She glanced at the museum's doors. "Maybe the hosts can help us make sense of why this ship would cause so much trouble."

Priscilla nodded. "I'm hopeful they can. And Wanda is definitely ready to meet Cherish and Tim."

"She's always liked the limelight."

"Really?"

April nodded. "You should have seen her ten years ago when she participated in a community talent show. She dressed like she was some big-screen movie siren from the 1930s. It was a hoot."

Priscilla waved to Gail and the young men. Gerald helped Wanda from the car and then carried her up the stairs while the two track stars carried the wheelchair up and into the museum. Wanda preened like a peacock, waving at the people waiting on the porch. Priscilla carried the ship.

"Look at this fine escort. The famous treatment has already started." Wanda patted Gerald's arm as color flamed up his face.

April rolled her eyes, then looked at Priscilla with a see-what-I-mean look on her face. Priscilla just grinned and led the way up the stairs. When Wanda's entourage entered, Cherish looked up from where she rested on the parlor's antique couch.

She smiled and stood. "You wouldn't believe how good it feels to sit on days like today." Cherish reached out a hand to Wanda, as Aidan pushed her forward in the wheelchair. "You must be Wanda Shire."

"I am." The older woman tittered and covered her heart with her hand as she lowered her chin. "Do you have a minute to look at something I brought?"

"For one of our dearest fans? Of course." Cherish smiled and gestured toward the table that had been set up in the center of the room. Priscilla set the ship on it.

"How did you get this ship?" Cherish's words trembled as she studied it.

Wanda shrugged from her seat in the wheelchair. "It was left in my cottage. We've tried to find the ship's owner, but haven't had any luck, so it's mine by default."

Cherish turned to Priscilla. "Did you know you called me about this ship already?"

Priscilla frowned as she looked at the host. "Me? How would I have done that?"

"My real name is Margie Throne. Cherish is a nickname my grandma gave me that's stuck. And it's been a nice on-camera name." She shifted her focus to Wanda. "My family spent an enjoyable week in the Relic last summer. It was such a charming cottage."

"Thank you. I think it's special."

"You are absolutely right. So you found this ship in the cottage?"

"I didn't." Wanda pointed at Priscilla. "She found it for me. This leg"—she thumped it with her fist—"hasn't allowed me to get around easily. But Gail and Priscilla were kind enough to look through the cottage for me." She leaned closer as if to share a secret. "I needed an excuse to come to the show and meet you. Unfortunately, when they showed me the ship, I'd never seen it before. There's something about it that's grown on me though. I'd like to know more about it."

"I can see why." Margie admired the ship and ran a hand lightly along the side. "And have you found out anything about it?"

Wanda looked to Priscilla, who tried to ignore the camera that was in the room. "I've talked to a lot of people this week, but no one's really been able to tell me anything about the ship. Someone suggested it could have come from Boston, but I don't know anything." She met Margie's gaze. "I talked to Bob Gothard and Shondra Johnson."

"So you took my advice and called them?"

"I didn't call them. Willow Gibson from here on the island looked at the ship for me, but isn't an expert on model ships. She suggested she could consult a few of her contacts, and I passed those two names on to her."

"Were they helpful?"

"Not like I'd hoped, but I have seen Bob Gothard on the island."

"Interesting. Sometimes he follows our show. Has a habit of showing up wherever we are."

Priscilla was willing to bet he didn't intimidate others everywhere he went though. "I think he's been up to more than that."

Cherish nodded as she eased the ship from one side to the other. "Items like this can be tricky to identify and place in the correct context. I'm afraid this one has me stumped. I haven't seen a ship like this before, although I think it would probably date around the early twentieth century."

Priscilla nodded enthusiastically and waved in Gerald's direction. "That's what Gerald—Captain Gerald O'Bannon—said also. It's a lightship—used in dangerous places too far offshore for a lighthouse to be effective."

Margie smiled at her. "You've done your homework."

Priscilla blushed, hoping the star of the show wasn't upset that a viewer had known something she didn't. "There's something inside, but we can't find a way to open the ship to get at whatever it is." She looked from the ship back to Margie. "There has to be a way, but I couldn't find it."

Margie stared at her, startled. "But I didn't—" Then she seemed to recover. "Let's see what we can find." She waved at Anna. "Bring the camera closer. In similar ships, I've seen hinged panels. Sometimes they're hidden, and other times it's a bit easier." She ran her fingers lightly over the surface, then slowed as she reached the helm. "This seems a little loose. Let's see if there's a reason." She lightly tugged at it and smiled. "All right."

Wanda squealed and leaned closer. "What did you find?"

CHAPTER TWENTY-NINE

I'll take that." A gruff voice caused Margie to jerk, and the helm popped up. With the force of the movement the ship slipped to its side, and Priscilla saw a small scrap of paper fall from it.

She dropped to the ground and reached for it.

Wanda squealed as someone tugged her wheelchair backward.

Priscilla's fingers closed around the paper. She kept her fist tightly closed around it and pushed herself up off her knees.

Before Priscilla fully straightened up, Bob Gothard pressed his way into the fray and snatched the ship from Margie. He couldn't slip away before April had a hand on him with Gerald taking Bob's other side.

"All right, sir. You've got some explaining to do." April kept her grip on the man and looked at Priscilla. "Could you call Chief Westin for me?"

"I sure can." Priscilla placed the call, then turned to Margie. "Did you know about this?"

"I did."

"How?" Priscilla noted that the cameraman held the camera focused on them.

"Last summer when my family and I were here, I noticed Bob hanging around. I knew who he was because we run in the same circles. I noticed him coming out of different cottages, but they were ones that seemed to be unoccupied. And I never saw him involved in any activities—he never swam in the ocean or walked on the beach or even just laid in the sun. It wouldn't be crazy for us both to be staying on the Camp Meeting grounds at the same time, but he'd be staying in one cottage, not several. It didn't feel right."

"You don't know what you're talking about." Bob kept his shoulders back, but his gaze shifted all over the place, as if he couldn't commit to meeting anyone's gaze. It made him look guilty of something.

April leaned toward him. "What were you doing on the island?"

"What everyone else does. Vacationing."

"What were you doing in the cottages?"

"Visiting friends. That's not a crime." He had a flash of attitude, and Priscilla almost wanted to warn him to stop talking before he implicated himself. But she knew the best way to catch him was to let him keep talking. Eventually he'd slip.

Priscilla turned to Margie. "So what did you do?"

"I tried to imagine what Bob would want with the cabins. He fancies himself an antiques expert, but really he just sells old toys at excessive prices."

"Hey, wait a minute," Bob sputtered, but Margie kept going.

"So I knew I needed to learn more about what he was up to. I wasn't sure how to do that. But then I saw him having a conversation with the woman who worked in the association office. He was comparing calendars with her." She smiled as she brushed a hand along the ship. "I overheard them talking about when the cottages were vacant, and how many he needed to 'hide' things in. It got me thinking about some high-priced antiques and toys that had gone missing on the mainland. Maybe he was using his toy website as a front to hide what he was really doing."

"And what's that?" Bob struggled to pull free but failed.

Priscilla answered his question. "Hiding stolen goods until it was safe to sell them. By working with Renee, you knew which cottages weren't owner-occupied. If you slipped items into those, chances were good no one would notice, since only the owner would know what belonged. Renee would tell you when a cottage was empty. And then you could clear things from one and add them to another."

Priscilla nodded as it all lined up with her theory. "So is this really a model ship from a valuable private collection?"

Margie shook her head. "No. My husband and I worked this scheme up between us. We planted the ship in the cabin before we left the island. We rolled it up in a blanket and stuffed it in a drawer in one of the bedrooms. We put some old wooden toys in there also. Then I talked to Tim and got Martha's Vineyard on the production schedule for the show. I sent Wanda a postcard telling her there might be something in the cabin that would work for the show, hoping she'd get in there and find the ship. When you called me about it, I did my best to get you to call Shondra. I'd asked her to tell you about this anonymous family. Shondra also told Bob that same story, and then I knew it was only a matter of coming here and waiting for him to make his move."

Wanda tapped her hands on the wheelchair. "What I don't understand is why? Why use Martha's Vineyard to hide valuable toys? This island isn't exactly accessible."

"It gives them a place for the goods to disappear while people forget about them." Priscilla could see the way it would make sense. "And then the goods can be sold after enough time has passed."

"You don't know what you're talking about." Bob tugged again, then slumped when no one released him. "Nobody was hurt."

"But why did you break into my house?" Priscilla watched him closely.

The man's forehead crinkled, and he pulled his head back as he straightened. "I don't know what you're talking about."

April put handcuffs on him. "Renee Overman's been filling that one in for us. That was her idea to get the ship back when Bob here started pressuring her for it. She made Jerry Shire tell her when you were at Wanda's, and she told this guy. It's one reason Jerry's been on the island so much."

Wanda put a hand over her heart. "My Jerry? He was involved?"

April shook her head. "We honestly don't know if he knew or if Renee took advantage of a relationship she cultivated with him. They were renting the cottage without your knowledge a couple or more weeks a year. But beyond that, I'm not sure yet what he knew." She tugged on Bob Gothard's arm. "Time to get you to the station where we can unravel the rest of this with our friends in

Boston. There are some property crime detectives who are very interested in talking to you."

"Thanks for all your help, Officer Brown." Priscilla watched Gothard resist being taken from the museum, but between April and Gerald, he didn't have much of a chance. After he was out of the way, she turned back to Wanda. "Well, it looks like we have part of our story."

"We know why the ship was in my cottage." But her lower lip trembled. "Now I don't know if Jerry was part of this mess or not." She rubbed her hand over her chest. "I think my heart might be breaking."

"Don't jump to conclusions yet." Priscilla glanced to where her cousin leaned against the wall.

Gail stepped forward and rubbed Wanda's arm. "We'll get it all figured out. Look at how much unraveled in the last twenty minutes."

"I just don't want Jerry raveled up in it."

"You heard Officer Brown." Priscilla moved to Wanda's other side. "There's a good chance Renee used him, and he didn't know what was happening. You have to trust the police to find the answer. You've lived here longer than I have, so you know they will."

"It's true." Wanda swallowed, and her quivering stopped. "I'll still have to decide what to do about his deceit."

"Yes." Gail squeezed her arm. "But God will give you wisdom. Sometimes it's grace and mercy, and other times it's tough love. He knows what Jerry needs."

"I know he won't stay at the campground this summer. I'll rent his week to recoup some of what he took." Wanda nodded decisively and turned back to Margie. "So what happens to the ship now?"

Margie closed the opening in the ship and handed it to Wanda. "The ship model is worth about two thousand dollars. That's what you'd get on the market. It's yours, Wanda. It more than paid for what I wanted to get out of it."

While Wanda regally accepted the crowd's congratulations, Priscilla stepped away and turned her back. Slowly, she opened her fist and spread out the piece of paper to read the one word written on it. *Vineyard.*

CHAPTER THIRTY

Background noise faded away as Priscilla stared at the slip of paper. Vineyard? As in Martha's Vineyard? What did it mean?

She was still pondering, lost in thought, when she heard Gerald's voice in her ear. "Looks like we have one last mystery to clear up, doesn't it?"

She leaned back into his sturdy chest, and he wrapped his arms around her. "What could it mean, Gerald?"

"I don't know, but I know where I can find out. Are you committed to being here for Mildred the rest of the day?"

Priscilla groaned. "I am. Oh, Gerald, I don't think I can take one more day of suspense. Could you find out...please?"

Gerald kissed the top of her head. "Text me the minute you're done here, and I'll get takeout, pick you up, take you home, and tell you whatever I find out. Deal?"

Priscilla turned in his arms. "Deal."

Gerald kissed her cheek. "So you'll text me?"

She laughed. "Count on it."

Six hours later, Priscilla had just enough strength to pull out her phone and text one word. *Now.* She needed home, food, sweet iced tea, a comfortable chair, information, and Gerald. Not necessarily in that order. When Gerald pulled up to the curb she didn't even wait for him to open the door for her as was his custom. She hauled herself into the front seat. "If you've ever loved me, you'll drive me away from here."

In answer, Gerald put the pedal to the metal and made it to the cottage in record time. It took a bowl of clam chowder and two glasses of sweet tea before Priscilla felt human again. She and Gerald put their feet up on the coffee table, and she told him about her *American Antiques* adventure. "I don't know how Tim and Cherish stay so fresh-looking, Gerald. Those hot lights, and all the takes they have to do over, the people sure they have a treasure who are disappointed when they find out their great-grandmother exaggerated its worth. And they do it all on their feet, and they never stop smiling. If it's an act, it's a good one."

Gerald took her hand. "I can't say I'm sorry to see the back end of their bus. Although I think what they brought to us is very special. I hope you'll think so too. Are you ready to hear the answers to our questions?"

Priscilla nodded.

Gerald stood. "I have a story to tell you, and I can only tell it to you in the lighthouse. If you can't walk there, I can give you a piggyback ride." He held his hand out to her.

Priscilla groaned, and stood. "I think if you did that, you'd be the one not able to make it to the lighthouse." She took his hand. "I think I have just enough strength to make it that far."

They walked in silence to the lighthouse door. Gerald unlocked it and pushed it open. He reached for the light switch and flipped it on before motioning to her to precede him inside. They settled in a couple of chairs he must have set up while she was at the museum.

Gerald took her hand again. "The lightship known as *Number 73* was built in 1901 and was positioned near Cape Cod from 1902 to 1924. From what I can tell, in 1924 it was given the name *Vineyard* and moved to the western end of Cuttyhunk Island to warn ships coming into the Sow and Pigs Reef." He raised his eyebrows. "Which, by the way, is a fascinating subject in itself. Cuttyhunk Island has fifty-two residents, and a school with three students. Incredibly hard to imagine.

"In September of 1944, the Great Atlantic Hurricane hit the east coast. The *Vineyard* survived the front of the storm. When the eye of the storm passed over the island, the lighthouse keeper clearly saw the lightship from the tower, and he and his family rejoiced, thinking the ship was saved. But the back of the hurricane hit about ten minutes later, and the *Vineyard* disappeared. It went down, taking all twelve crew members down with her. The wreckage wasn't found until almost nineteen years to the day after she sank, almost a mile from where she went down.

"The divers salvaged the bell from the *Vineyard,* and after a couple of false starts, fifty-five years to the day after the *Vineyard's* sinking, the bell was commemorated in a ceremony that honored the sacrifices of the men of the *Vineyard* lightship."

When Gerald stopped speaking, Priscilla realized her cheeks were wet with tears. They were silent for a few minutes, and she knew Gerald was thinking of the men and women he'd known who had given their lives for others on the sea.

Finally she broke the silence. "Does Wanda know? Did you tell her?"

Gerald stood and drew her up with him. "No, I didn't."

Priscilla frowned at him. "But don't you think she should know? Don't you think the owner of the ship should know the story of the *Vineyard's* crew?"

Gerald smiled and gazed into her eyes. "She does know."

"But you just said—"

"I said the owner of the ship knows." He took her by the shoulders and slowly turned her around so she was facing the half-empty display case that held a couple of navigation tools she'd found in the lighthouse. But it wasn't half-empty anymore. There was the *Vineyard,* behind protective glass, with a placard that told its story.

Priscilla was speechless. Then she broke into fresh tears. "Gerald, how? It's too wonderful."

Gerald took her in his arms. He put his forehead to hers. "Priscilla. Do you think I would pass up a chance to give you something your heart desired so badly? You fell in love with that lightship before you knew its story. I would have paid Wanda much more than she ended up asking for it. This is where it belongs. Its place is here."

Priscilla dried her tears, laughing with delight and gratitude. To Gerald, for knowing her heart and giving her his. And to God, who knew her heart best of all and was giving her the most thoughtful and wonderful Coast Guard captain that ever walked the earth.

CHAPTER THIRTY-ONE

Sunday afternoon, Priscilla glanced around her yard and smiled. This was going to be a perfect day for Uncle Hugh and Marigold's wedding. The clouds skated across a bright blue sky, and the breeze off the bay was just enough to keep the air moving without causing a disruption or messing up the guests' hair.

Gerald and Tommy tag-teamed as they raced to get the arbor Marigold had requested installed before guests arrived.

Priscilla glanced at her watch. It was already one, but they should have sufficient time to finalize the rest of the details for the bridal couple.

The flowers looked beautiful, thriving from the long drink of water she'd given them the prior night. The plants looked vibrant, and with the sun ducking behind occasional clouds, the weather was almost perfect.

It had turned into a beautiful day for the long-awaited wedding.

Gail and Trudy were looping bunting down the center aisle chairs. The look was charming, separating the two sections and marking the walkway for Marigold. Priscilla chuckled as she remembered overhearing the bride telling her pastor she didn't plan to stand for more than ten minutes, so he was to keep his remarks quick and to the point. She and Hugh did not have time to waste on "flowery extras."

Her pastor had looked a little stunned, but Priscilla admired Marigold's gumption and honesty. She had definitely earned the right to know what she wanted. The woman had taken up residence in Priscilla's bedroom, so her granddaughter could beautify her without Uncle Hugh being any the wiser. Slowly the lawn filled with friends and family. They found seats on the white folding chairs, and the soft murmur of their conversations filled the yard.

Precisely at two, Uncle Hugh walked out of the lighthouse with the pastor and Tommy. Priscilla's uncle looked spiffy in his best church suit and sporting a fresh haircut. She stifled a giggle as she spotted what might even be a spot of toilet paper on his cheek where he'd cut himself shaving.

Joan turned to her with a raised eyebrow, but Priscilla waved her away. The breeze might whisk it away before anyone else noticed. There was a pause, then Trudy hit a button on a CD player, and the strains of Pachelbel's *Canon in D* began to flow.

Gail emerged from the cottage, followed by Marigold, who wore a deep red dress that looked like it might have been a mother- or grandmother-of-the-bride dress. It was stunning, providing a sharp contrast to Marigold's snowy-white hair and cornflower-blue eyes.

When Priscilla returned her attention to her uncle, it was clear he was as smitten as a young groom with his bride. He had eyes only for Marigold as she glided down the grass between the rows of chairs.

While Uncle Hugh and Marigold were sweet as they exchanged vows, Priscilla's focus kept getting drawn to Gail and the way she looked at Tommy. Maybe now her cousin would finally embrace her own future with the man she loved.

Then Priscilla's gaze collided with Gerald's. He winked at her, and she felt tingles all the way down her spine to the bottom of her feet.

That man had captured her heart. And as the reception began, she breathed in each moment and promised herself she would remember every detail.

Because every one of them was worth savoring.

AUTHOR LETTER

Dear Reader,

There's something about returning to the island of Martha's Vineyard that feels like coming home. Each time I open a blank document to start a new book, I can see the characters, the communities, and the beach.

This time I had the pleasure of researching and learning about the ways that the community honors and celebrates Memorial Day. The school events as depicted in this story are accurate and reflect what the community does. And it was interesting to research antique toys and the hidden value we find in them. While it was fun for me to research them, Priscilla didn't have fun trying to unlock the story of the ship. The story of the *Vineyard* lightship took place just as Gerald related it. One of the reasons we know this is because of the five-year-old daughter of the lighthouse keeper on Cuttyhunk Island. She grew up and wrote a book about life as a lighthouse keeper's daughter and vividly recalls the night the Great Atlantic Hurricane claimed 344 lives at sea, including the entire crew of the *Vineyard*.

While Priscilla was trying to find the story, she was reminded of how frustrating it can be when people won't answer questions.

Renee was trying so hard to hide what was going on at the Camp Meeting Association, but truth won in the end.

If you haven't done any research about the cottages at the Camp Meeting grounds, you really should. They are charming and look like oversized dollhouses. The insides are small, but cute as well. They look like a wonderful place to escape while on the island.

I hope you've enjoyed this return trip and exploration of Martha's Vineyard.

Blessings until next time,

Cara Putman

ABOUT THE AUTHOR

Cara Putman is the award-winning author of more than thirty novels. She lives in Indiana with her husband and four children, where she teaches law at a Big Ten university business school and is active in her community and church. When she isn't writing or teaching, Cara loves to read and spend time outdoors with her family. You can learn more about Cara and her books at http://www.caraputman.com.

AN ARMCHAIR TOUR OF
MARTHA'S VINEYARD

The Martha's Vineyard Camp Meeting Association

The Martha's Vineyard Camp Meeting Association is a National Historic Landmark that has been part of the island since 1844. Camp meetings were held on the island earlier than that, but in 1835 a group selected the location of the current Camp Meeting Association. It was a tent camp from 1844 until the cottages began to be constructed in the post-Civil War era. In 1864 a plot of twenty-six acres was purchased for the camp.

When the cottages were constructed, they were built on the same locations as the tents. This is one reason they are huddled together in clusters. The doors are actually located where the doors of the tents were.

The iron Tabernacle is the centerpiece of the grounds and has been in use since 1879. It is still used for services and concerts. The cottages are what drew me to this area though. They are each unique, and the colors create a lovely rainbow effect.

If you're ever on the island be sure to stop and walk the grounds. You can take a tour and visit the museum as well.

SOMETHING DELICIOUS FROM
OUR SEASIDE FRIENDS

Seashell Cookies
(Perfect for an Ocean-View Wedding Reception!)

Ingredients:

For a realistic-looking yet edible "sand" base:

2 14.3 oz. pkgs.	Vanilla sandwich cookies, such as Golden Oreos
4 cookies	Chocolate sandwich cookies, such as chocolate Oreos, (could be taken from package for dipped cookies listed below, if chocolate cookies are the ones chosen for dipping.)

For molded seashell cookie toppers:

2 12-oz. pkgs.	White candy-melt wafers

For dipped cookies:

1 19.1 oz. pkg.	Sandwich cookies in the flavor of your choice.

2 12-oz. pkgs.	Candy-melt wafers in your preferred color. These are available in a wide variety of colors at local grocery stores, party-supply stores, or online.

Items You Will Need:

Seashell-shaped candy mold. Available online or at local craft-supply stores.

Instructions:

Seashell Toppers: Melt the white candy-melt wafers in the microwave in 30-second increments, stirring in between, until thoroughly melted and smooth. A half-teaspoon of shortening can be added if the texture is too dry. (Usually no more than one minute of cooking time is required.) You may also use the stovetop or a chocolate melter if you prefer. Pour melted mixture into seashell candy mold. Place in the fridge while you continue making the cookies. Once seashells are hard, remove from fridge and pop out of mold, setting aside on a plate or a sheet of waxed paper.

Sand: Place all the vanilla sandwich cookies in a food processor with the four chocolate ones. Pulse until texture resembles sand. Reserve for your display platter.

Dipped Cookies: Melt the colored candy melts in the same manner you melted the white wafers for the seashell toppers. Dip each sandwich cookie in the colored candy melts and tap off excess. Place on a piece of waxed paper. Immediately press a seashell into the candy-covered sandwich cookie before it hardens. This will hold the seashell in place. Continue dipping and placing seashells onto the dipped sandwich cookies until the desired number of cookies have been covered. Allow cookies time to harden, then remove from waxed paper and "bury" the cookies in the edible sand, which you've spread over a platter or tray.

Read on for a sneak peek of another exciting book
in the Mysteries of Martha's Vineyard series!

Waves of Doubt
by Nancy Mehl with Shaen Layle

Priscilla took a deep breath, grabbed the folder, and got out of her car, taking a moment to smooth her wrinkled blouse and capris. Then she began walking toward the lovely house. She was struck again by the beauty of its gorgeous Queen Anne craftsmanship, both solid and delicately ornate at once. Situated just outside of Tisbury, it was surrounded by trees, hard to see from the road, and very isolated. Priscilla had heard rumors that Virginia Lawrence was thinking about selling, but she had no idea if the gossip was true. She'd only met the elusive historian once before today, when she'd set up the lecture. Priscilla's cousin, Joan Abernathy, had recruited her to snag Virginia for the summer series at the library.

"You're so much better with people than I am," she'd said. "I'm sure she'll agree to speak at the library if you ask her."

Priscilla considered herself much too tactful to point out that a past unfortunate comment, made many years ago by Joan at a History Tea sponsored by the museum, had driven a wedge between the two women. Joan never shared the actual comment, but it must have been a doozy to produce such a longstanding rift.

As Priscilla approached the front door, it suddenly swung open. Virginia Lawrence stood there in all her peculiar glory. Bright red hair in a shade not actually seen in nature was piled high on top of her head. The mound of hair, obviously a wig, tipped so precariously to one side that Priscilla worried it would topple over. Virginia's eyebrows, drawn on with black pencil, arched on her forehead, making her look permanently surprised. One hand extended from underneath her bright red cape, which was a fashion accessory worn by the unconventional historian on all occasions, regardless of the weather. June on the Vineyard usually ranged in the 70s or 80s, but no matter how hot it got, Virginia's cape stayed in place.

"Is that it?" Virginia asked in her nasal voice. She pointed at the folder Priscilla held in her hands.

"Yes, it is," Priscilla said with a smile.

Virginia swung the door all the way open. "Please bring it in."

Priscilla suddenly felt as if the folder she had brought was the guest and she was nothing more than a delivery driver carrying precious cargo. She followed her hostess into a large living room decorated with furniture and artwork that matched the style of the house. It was tastefully done, which surprised Priscilla. Virginia looked sadly out of place in the gracious room.

"Have a seat," the elderly woman said, waving her hand toward a rose-colored brocade couch. "Would you like some lemonade?"

A pitcher and two glasses waited on a silver tray placed on a carved mahogany table in front of the couch.

"Thank you," Priscilla said as she took a seat. "That sounds nice."

At that moment, a large Irish setter came galloping into the room. He ran right up to Priscilla and sat down in front of her.

"Magnus, don't bother the woman." Although Virginia's words were a rebuke, her voice was gentle. It was clear the dog was special to her.

"He's not bothering me," Priscilla said. She stroked the soft fur on the setter's head. Magnus rewarded her with a sloppy smile. "I have a dog too. His name is Jake."

For a moment, the elderly woman's self-important expression slipped, and a softness came into her eyes. "I don't know what I'd do without Magnus," she said. "He's my best friend." As if suddenly remembering she had a guest, she cleared her throat and poured two glasses of lemonade.

"We've had a lot of interest in your lecture," Priscilla said, taking the glass held out to her. "I think we'll have peak attendance."

Virginia stared at Priscilla as if cucumbers had suddenly sprouted from her ears. "Of course we will. I have quite a following. I assumed you knew that."

Although Priscilla suspected the featured topic of Nancy Luce was the main reason for interest in the lecture, she had to admit that the whole town was buzzing over the fact that Virginia might actually make a public appearance after all these years. Though she'd lived on the island most of her life, she was notoriously reclusive. And yet, Nancy Luce held a great deal of local fascination in her own right. The quirky historical figure native to the Island, known as the "Chicken Lady," Luce lived her entire life at her farmhouse near the head of Tiah's Cove in West Tisbury. She cared for her parents until they died, and raised animals, including the chickens she named and loved. She was a folk artist, poet, businesswoman, and writer. Some considered her to be the first female entrepreneur on the Island.

Priscilla raised the glass of lemonade to her lips, giving herself a moment to regroup. She almost gasped at the sourness of the drink. Virginia was also known as a tightwad. It appeared sugar was on her list of luxuries. Priscilla put the glass down on the table and forced a smile for the starchy woman. Magnus, who seemed to have grown tired of staring at Priscilla, lay down on top of her feet.

"Would it kill you to use a coaster?" Virginia pointed a scarlet fingernail at Priscilla. "I assume you weren't raised in a barn. Though, coming from Kansas…" She trailed off, one eyebrow raised.

Priscilla shot Virginia another tight smile and looked for a coaster. Not finding one, she placed her napkin underneath her sweating glass. She looked longingly toward the front door.

She exhaled slowly in an attempt to steady her nerves and picked up the folder. She untied it and carefully withdrew a small journal. "Here is the most recent discovery, Nancy's diary. Mildred told me it was found in an attic in an old house in West Tisbury."

Virginia sniffed. "As the preeminent scholar of Nancy Luce's life and accomplishments, I truly believe I should be the keeper of her legacy. I have said this to Mildred Pearson many times, to no avail. Why that woman has been trusted with the care of the East Shore Historical Museum is beyond me." She took the diary from Priscilla.

Priscilla withdrew the rest of the folder's contents—letters and photographs, all encased in plastic sleeves. "Here are some pictures of Nancy and her chickens." She put the pictures in front of Virginia, who picked up the photos as if she were touching something sacred.

"Teeddla Toona, Levendy Ludandy, and Otte Opheto," Virginia said in a breathless tone.

"Excuse me?" Priscilla asked with alarm. Was Virginia having a stroke?

Virginia glared at Priscilla. "The names of some of her chickens. Don't you know anything about Nancy Luce?" She shook her head. "Really, if you want to work with people like me, you need to educate yourself." She sighed deeply, obviously pushed to her limits having to deal with a moron like Priscilla.

"I may not know the names of her chickens, but I know she was a very independent lady who made a name for herself because of her creativity and resilience. Like you, Virginia." Priscilla tossed her another smile even though it hurt. "I'm glad you'll be able to use these artifacts for your lecture. Mildred will meet you after the presentation tonight to pick them up. She asked me to remind you that they are on loan from the New England History Museum in Boston and should be returned in pristine condition." Priscilla stood, which took some talent since she had to regain the use of her feet. Thankfully, Magnus cooperated and scooted over. "I really must be going, but I'll see you this evening at the library."

Virginia pushed herself up from the sofa, trying not to trip over her dog. "I-I really do appreciate the chance to view these items before tonight. I will most certainly incorporate them into my lecture, and I'll guard them closely until this evening. You have my word." She stuck her hand out. "Thank you, Priscilla."

Priscilla shook Virginia's hand, wondering what had happened to make her soften her stance. Maybe she wasn't quite as obnoxious as Priscilla had assumed. "You're welcome, Virginia. I'm really looking forward to tonight."

"Of course you are, dear. I hope I can bring a spark into your dull existence."

Priscilla turned and headed for the front door and freedom. "Your home is beautiful," she said, attempting to fill the awkward silence.

"Yes, it is," Virginia said. "I'll miss it."

Priscilla turned to look at her. The rumors must be true. "Miss it? Are you leaving?"

Virginia nodded. "I've actually sold the property. I'm moving to Boston. I'm ready to leave this dreary little town behind me. *My kind of people live in Boston, and I want to be a part of something bigger. I'm sure you understand.*" She gazed at her beautiful garden through the large windows that lined one side of the room and sighed. "Besides, my nephew, Douglas, needs some help with his play. I promised to invest in it, and selling the house has allowed me to assist him. He's putting it on at the Playhouse, you know. *Murder by Moonlight.*"

Priscilla nodded. "My cousin, Trudy Galvin, has a starring role. She's very excited about it. Loves the play."

"Yes, she would. It's very good. I hope she has some talent. I would hate to see his play destroyed by amateurish hacks."

Priscilla swallowed hard. "I'd better go. I'll see you tonight." She almost ran out to her car. When she got inside, she gripped the steering wheel and waited until her pounding heart began to beat normally.

She spent the rest of the afternoon helping Mildred and Clara, the head librarian, prepare for the lecture. They decorated the library's largest conference room with poster-sized excerpts from Nancy's diary and black-and-white portraits of her beloved chickens. Linen-covered tables lined the perimeter, offering a catered spread of delicious-smelling treats from Candy Lane Confectionary. The display nearest Priscilla held a new confection from Candy—rosewater petits fours—studded judiciously with cranberries. They smelled heavenly, and Pricilla's mouth watered.

But this was no time for treats. They still had to put the chairs in place. Judging from the registration list, the room's 112-person capacity was going to be stretched to its limits. Priscilla worked until she was starting to perspire a little and had to fan the collar of her blouse to cool herself off. She was surveying their work when she heard someone call her name.

She looked up to see Joan striding purposefully toward her.

"Hi, Joan. What are you doing here so early? The event doesn't start for another forty-five minutes."

"Tell that to the mob of people waiting out front. There's even a news crew here." She snorted. "They probably think they're going to get a rare interview with the town's Havisham."

Priscilla grinned at Joan's reference to the mad Miss Havisham from Dickens's novel, *Great Expectations*. There were definite similarities between Virginia and the wildly eccentric character.

Joan glanced around the room appraisingly. "We're going to need more seating."

Clara led the women to another room that held a few more chairs. Priscilla, Mildred, and Joan had just set them up when Clara opened the door and let the crowd in. Priscilla was surprised to see Dr. Ava Pennywhistle, Virginia's chief rival for the coveted title of the Vineyard's number one historian. Virginia and Ava disliked each other intensely, but there was Ava slipping into a chair on the back row. She certainly didn't look happy.

Priscilla was also intrigued to see several women in long white dresses enter the room. The women in white. She'd heard about them from Mildred. A group dedicated to keeping Nancy Luce's legacy alive. Frankly, Priscilla found them odd. Their devotion to the long-deceased "chicken lady" seemed more than a little eccentric.

A few minutes later, Priscilla's cousin Gail walked through the door. Joan went over to meet her, and they took their seats on the third row, saving a seat for Trudy, who was in rehearsals at the Playhouse. She'd promised to come as soon as she got out.

Mildred sat down on the front row, probably so she could keep a close eye on the Nancy Luce items. As soon as the lecture was over, she planned to return them immediately to the museum.

Priscilla smiled to herself as she scanned the room, watching for Gerald, her handsome Coast Guard captain. He finally showed up at six, just when the lecture was supposed to start. But where was Virginia?

At ten minutes after six, Priscilla started to perspire in earnest. Sweat, actually. The news crew was getting antsy. If Virginia didn't show up soon, they would probably leave. Five minutes later, Priscilla left the buzz of the crowd to call Virginia. She found an empty hallway and pulled her cell phone out of her purse. She didn't expect Virginia to still be at home, but what if she had taken ill at the last minute? Priscilla didn't have a mobile number for her and suspected she didn't own a cell phone. The landline rang and rang, until it finally clicked over to an answering machine with a crabby-sounding recording of Virginia deriding telemarketers and solicitors, followed by an ear-piercing beep.

"Hello? Virginia? It's Priscilla Grant. You have quite a large crowd gathered at the library. I was just—um—checking to make sure you weren't ill or something. Please call me back." With a sigh, Priscilla ended the call. If Virginia didn't show up, what on earth was she going to say to all these people? Although she'd tried to ignore them, some of the skeptical comments from the audience had reached her ears.

After several more calls to Virginia's house with no success, the reality of the situation hit Priscilla. Virginia wasn't coming. It was possible she'd changed her mind, but mere hours earlier, she'd seemed genuinely interested in leading the lecture.

In her gut, Priscilla knew something was wrong. Virginia wasn't here.

And neither were the museum's artifacts.

A NOTE FROM THE EDITORS

We hope you enjoyed Mysteries of Martha's Vineyard, published by the Books and Inspirational Media Division of Guideposts, a nonprofit organization that touches millions of lives every day through products and services that inspire, encourage, help you grow in your faith, and celebrate God's love.

Thank you for making a difference with your purchase of this book, which helps fund our many outreach programs to military personnel, prisons, hospitals, nursing homes, and educational institutions.

We also create many useful and uplifting online resources. Visit Guideposts.org to read true stories of hope and inspiration, access OurPrayer network, sign up for free newsletters, download free e-books, join our Facebook community, and follow our stimulating blogs.

To learn about other Guideposts publications, including the best-selling devotional *Daily Guideposts*, go to Guideposts.org/Shop, call (800) 932-2145, or write to Guideposts, PO Box 5815, Harlan, Iowa 51593.

Sign up for the
Guideposts Fiction Newsletter
and stay up-to-date on the books you love!

You'll get sneak peeks of new releases, recommendations from other Guideposts readers, and special offers just for you . . .

and it's FREE!

Just go to Guideposts.org/Newsletters today to sign up.

Guideposts.®

Visit Guideposts.org/Shop
or call (800) 932-2145

Find more inspiring fiction in these best-loved Guideposts series!

Secrets of Wayfarers Inn

Fall back in history with three retired schoolteachers who find themselves owners of an old warehouse-turned-inn that is filled with hidden passages, buried secrets and stunning surprises that will set them on a course to puzzling mysteries from the Underground Railroad.

Sugarcreek Amish Mysteries

Be intrigued by the suspense and joyful "aha" moments in these delightful stories. Each book in the series brings together two women of vastly different backgrounds and traditions, who realize there's much more to the "simple life" than meets the eye.

Tearoom Mysteries Series

Mix one stately Victorian home, a charming lakeside town in Maine, and two adventurous cousins with a passion for tea and hospitality. Add a large scoop of intriguing mystery and sprinkle generously with faith, family, and friends, and you have the recipe for *Tearoom Mysteries*.

Mysteries of Silver Peak

Escape to the historic mining town of Silver Peak, Colorado, and discover how one woman's love of antiques helps her solve mysteries buried deep in the town's checkered past.

**To learn more about these books,
visit Guideposts.org/Shop**